Also by William Palmer

The Good Republic

Leporello

The Contract

William Palmer

Four Last Things

Secker & Warburg
LONDON

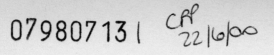

The author gratefully acknowledges permission to reproduce the
following copyright material:

Rimbaud – Selected Verse, edited by Oliver Bernard, Penguin Books,
1962; *Mysterious Britain*, by Janet and Colin Bord, Paladin, 1974;
Selected Poems, by John Crowe Ransom, Eyre and Spottiswoode,
1947.

He also wishes to thank the editors of the following magazines and
journals in which these stories, in sometimes slightly different
form, first appeared: *Critical Quarterly, Daily Telegraph, London
Magazine, Panurge* and *Stand*.

First published in Great Britain in 1996
by Martin Secker & Warburg Limited
an imprint of Reed International Books Limited
Michelin House, 81 Fulham Road, London SW3 6RB
and Auckland, Melbourne, Singapore and Toronto

A CIP catalogue record for this book
is available from the British Library

ISBN 0 436 36051 9

Typeset in Perpetua
by Deltatype Ltd, Ellesmere Port, Cheshire
Printed and bound in Great Britain by
Clays Ltd, St Ives plc

Contents

Four Last Things

Cornelius Marten pushed through the high doors of Broadcasting House in a bad temper and headed straight for the George. Ten years since he had been in here. One drink only, he said to himself. A large whisky. A pint of beer. Two more whiskies. To his astonishment he saw that it was nearly seven o'clock. Unrecognized by anyone in the pub, he went to another, anonymous, then another, and another, getting progressively less aggrieved by the sight of the elderly little man who stared out at him from the bar mirrors. He caught a taxi to home, but stopped the driver short on Highgate Hill and went into a pub he did not know at all except from its outside. It was blessedly half-empty, the late summer night dying in the engraved windows. The girls who served him with several more drinks seemed to have been on a course of some sort; every time they handed him change or a glass they said, with broad, empty smiles, 'Thanks. There you go then.' A minor irritation, but yet another to add to the long list.

Drunk, he was convinced he did not show any signs of it; all his life he had had a great capacity for drink; for his generation it had been the fuel of creativity. How could he ever have produced that great quintet of novels without the help of the bottle? Rimbaud, Joyce, Faulkner, Fitzgerald, Lowry – all came from the green and glassy, blood-red and amber, piss- and straw-coloured; crapulous and epiphanic, their greatest, clearest, most visionary moments bestowed by the world re-emerging, shining and pure and washed after excess. 'As soon as the idea of the Flood had subsided . . .' As he replaced his empty glass on the counter, Cornelius recognized an old acquaintance, a fellow-writer of his own generation, whose name he could not quite place . . . He began to talk familiarly to him, telling of his unsatisfactory visit to the BBC, the memorial broadcast to Spencer, the ridiculous charlatans he had been forced to share a table with, the young woman with large blue-framed spectacles who spoke in a curiously slovenly educated accent halfway between Edinburgh and Islington so that words were extruded between her thin, pursed lips like toffeed marbles, the Irishman with great grey blind eyes whose speech was passionate nonsense, the fat American, of residual and repulsive handsomeness; his own joke about a nuclear bombardment leaving them deep under London, the only . . . Only to be met with a series of increasingly puzzled stares, an 'I'm sorry, but – ', then a curt nod as the man turned his back rudely on him. Then, himself a horrified bystander, Cornelius found his mouth opening and exploding with a stream of obscenities, 'Bollocks. Shit. Piss,' shouted singly, very loudly, and with frightening emphasis. The girls froze and stared down the bar at him. Beer dribbled over the lip of the glass one held under a tap. And the man turned round, with the startled, angry face of a complete stranger.

He had never done anything like that before. What? He could not remember. He looked in terror across the breakfast table to Dorothy.

'Was I all right last night? Did I say anything to you?'

'You were drunk, if that's what you mean. I told you going into town was bad for you. You never listen.' She refolded the *Guardian* carefully.

'I didn't say anything?'

'You weren't making much sense. You kept going on about some man who insulted you in a pub.'

'I think I shall go back to bed. I feel most unwell.'

Dorothy shook the paper like a thundersheet.

For the rest of the week, he felt increasingly unwell. For two days he drank nothing, hoping he would recover his former balance, then convinced himself that the lack of alcohol was making his condition worse. There came a morning when he descended the stairs in a muffled haze of Scotch and sleeplessness. He was neatly dressed, in a dark suit, a tie, a blue and white striped shirt, but the matching stripes of his pyjamas protruded from the bottoms of his suit trouser-legs and broke over his black shoes. He passed, without looking at it, the usual freight of papers and post on the hall table.

Then he was entering the gates of Waterlow Park. Nothing and everything was as it should be. The park was edged fantastically against a grey, sagging sky. The small iron railings to lawns, like necklaces of joined croquet hoops, had been freshly painted black. Leaves on the gravel paths lay shining, flat and still. Mallards wearing blue and white medal ribbons floated unmoving on the oval ponds. From the trees, birds talked incessantly, tinny and querulous. The world was jerked to one side. As if he were suddenly walking down a steep incline, Cornelius teetered to the edge of the path, tripped, twisted in falling, and sat down heavily on the grass.

Then it was night and he was somewhere strange. How he had passed the intervening hours he did not know. Presumably, he thought with shame later, he had looked like a tramp or drunk or one of those poor, half-mad derelicts who lie, lumpy, dishevelled and broken, like fallen and disregarded statues in our public places now. He was aware of white and pale-blue cloth that hovered above his face, smelling sweetly clean. Of people probing gently about his body, their hands in his hands, in his pockets, tugging gently at his trousers, discovering his arms in the black tubes of his coat, hands fluttering about him, touching here and there, as if inferring the existence of his body from the filled-out costume. A white ceiling revolved, a long window frame slid down the wall and under the floor, a diagonal of brown door sailed on a blue pool. The hands of a green clock turned overhead. Then walls and ceiling and floor all came to rest. A voice said, 'You are in hospital.'

The next day two ambulancemen helped him up his own stairs. He felt incredibly reduced, in weight, height, *substance*.

'Bit of a mess, really,' said the doctor breezily. 'Had a black-out before like that? Warning sign at your age. Drink a lot? Get into your sixties – there's a progressive lack of tolerance. Bronchitis, too. Could have gone into pneumonia. Lucky.' He injected his silent patient.

Which, thought Cornelius, is one way of putting it.

The doctor turned his back and spoke to Dorothy as if Cornelius were not there.

The expected words – rest, warmth, take three of these a day after meals, no more than a unit of alcohol a day, the hand will mend – his left hand, broken in his fall.

'I thought you were dying,' said Dorothy quietly, when the doctor had gone.

Oh no, Cornelius thought, being disinclined to speak, death when it comes will be more than this, surely. Will announce itself.

He stayed in bed for three weeks, reading, fretting, dozing, developing that cinema in the head that was his chief consolation. Not, oh not, the nightmares that rode through his sleep. But these largely benign reveries of endless, dull conversations, of glimpses into strange rooms where people simply performed everyday acts, of chaste women disrobing – of himself receiving literary prizes.

But the initial euphoria of having survived, of rest and sobriety – he was allowed one glass of red wine an evening – soon began to pall. The weather darkened and so did his mood. He could no longer face the pile of green Penguin detective novels. He lay depressed and torpid. There must be spiritual comfort some-where. On Dorothy's cabinet, in her small pile of books, was another, thick paperback, *The Confessions of St Augustine*.

He tried to read the first page. It was tiring to hold a book with one hand. He laid it on the pillow and let his dead hand hold the pages down while his other, wetted index fingertip turned through looking for the sex he vaguely remembered. Instead, he came to a passage on friendship, grief at the death of a friend, and read: 'Time is not idle; its revolution is not without effect . . .'

Tears welled in his eyes. What of his friends? Why had no one come?

'Why does no one come?' he wailed to Dorothy. 'My friends? Spencer?'

'Spencer is dead, Cornelius. You know that he is. What an odd choice.'

So he was. So he was. Both dead, and an odd choice.

'I will get up,' he said decisively. 'Otherwise I shall die too.'

No one called, but he was downstairs, within reach of the radio. He refused Dorothy's offer of a television set, though she had a small black and white portable upstairs in her bedroom. It was one of the last remaining evidences of his mental superiority over her. He would read all the books he should have read. He had grown lazy in the head. That was why he could not write. He had become addicted to the fictive. Was there such a word? His next book would be autobiographical in nature. But not the usual romantic, subjective writer's autobiography. No – he wished to write the history of the evolution of a twentieth-century man's intellectual development. To show how he himself had evolved and matured beyond the early mechanistic, rational position of his youth and of his time, to the, well, to the quasi-religious position to which modern science and his own thought had brought him. Koestler had been scorned for his interest in what lay behind our dry explanation – but yes, there must be more. At this time, when Western thought was in a crisis, Art and personality were no longer enough. They had gone beyond that . . .

The books he asked Dorothy to get from the public library now were investigations of the new physics, the paranormal, and eastern religions that were endlessly welcoming, endlessly receding from sense. He sought for comfort in ideas he had once ridiculed. She said that the books were nonsense. Cornelius looked in them for what would confirm what he already thought. He ignored what contradicted him. His health improved. He worked an hour a day in his study, note-taking and reading.

But he still could not write. And slowly his fears began to grow again. He found concentration slipping away from him. Then, one gloomy morning, with the city outside his window – from this top room he could look down over the dull, dry, cancerous tumour of Highgate Hill – he decided that his only hope was to move from here. He would set Dorothy to look for a house in the country.

He day-dreamed that a new house would be his saving. He could start afresh. There would be no more drink; no more idle dreams of compliant women. He would be the Prospero of a magical island. Who was it, Tycho Brahe? who had lived in a palace on an island, surrounded by human grotesques and intricate and inaccurate images of Heaven and the heavens. Brahe had a silver nose – and Cornelius imagined him, himself, bent over calculations, candle-light lambent on his nose, listing in tiny black squiggles the permutations and perturbations of unimaginably distant, massive worlds.

Or no – spiritually and imaginatively refreshed, he would build – impossible – have built, find, refurbish, a house such as Jung had had built for himself. For hours Cornelius hunted through books to find a photograph he thought that he remembered. The outside walls of the house were white, impasto-spiked plaster like melted and re-hardened cake icing; inscriptions and cabbalistic signs were carved on the door lintels . . . He could not find the picture. Perhaps he had only dreamed it. More and more the two things, memory and imagination, became confused. Time to go. The thought of flight was intoxicating.

That was simply all that was needed. London, the city, was the poison that was draining his life away. They must move. They must be where he could breathe, move, think, work. He was stronger now. He would gain fresh strength from new surroundings.

He set Dorothy to look for a house in the country.

It took her a month.

They turned off the road where a signpost pointed on to DISS and down a narrow, straight, scrawnily hedged lane. Dorothy slowed after half a mile of flat landscape, braked too sharply, and then nosed the car into the drive of a large, redbrick, double-fronted Georgian house. Built onto its side was a long, incongruously white shoe box with a colonnade of grey pillars along its front-facing wall – Dorothy had pointed this out to him on a photograph and it was what had instantly decided him to take the house. The drive ran past its end. As they drove slowly past, Cornelius saw through the tall french windows the empty shelves running the length and height of the walls, the boxes and tea-chests of books on the floor. Dorothy pulled round and stopped. They got out of the car. The back of the house was a muddle of windows, crooked doors with rusty horseshoes nailed above them, the lines of dark-red bricks and yellow mortar more haphazard and rambling than those at the front.

After London, the silence was slightly unnerving. Cornelius hurried inside, homing as if by instinct through the strange, musty-smelling house, to the room he already called his library.

Every day is the same. Eleven o'clock. An hour, perhaps two passes as he stares blankly at the windows, the sparse birch copse at the end of the side garden disappearing when he blinks. The north light hangs between the now filled bookshelves. The slab of paper is untouched after two hours, only the phrase, *Every morning, my father*, substituted for the cancelled, *Every day, his father* . . . He does not feel like work. Work will wait. He crosses the room, takes down a book; only to leave it, unread, after a few words, abandoned on the desk or sofa or floor, as he wanders morosely out, along the corridor, up the stairs, into the bathroom, unbuttons, urinates, petulantly aborts the flush, re-buttons, tries again at the flush chain, grimaces into the mirror, comes back down the stairs, settles the door softly to behind him, picks up the book again.

It is not that Cornelius is idle. He has worked hard throughout his life; the row of his own books, the translations of them, make up two rows of one case. It is that something has ceased in him. Something that used to need satisfaction and in turn satisfied. He must, he must read. At least that.

Today it was a glossy paperback that Dorothy, on his instructions, had brought back from Cambridge on her last shopping trip. He poured out another large Scotch and topped it up with dusty water. He decided on the sofa; the desk was too prescriptive of work. He lay, supporting himself on one elbow. His good hand opened the book. A photograph of a tiny stone hut, somewhere in Ireland. The caption read – 'The whole building looks like an upturned boat. This shape may have a special purpose – to attract and concentrate the cosmic energies along the roof ridge, and then disperse them within the building, to the spiritual and physical benefit of anyone engaged in religious activity inside.'

Or to keep off the rain, the last of Cornelius's sense suggested. But he began to read the book.

The day wore away outside the window.

He must have slept. Somehow he had got onto the sofa. Dorothy was standing over him. Her face was a blur. He reached down to where his spectacles had fallen.

'I thought you were working or I would have come in earlier.' How many endless degrees of irony could be read in her cool tone. 'That was a Mr Pritchard on the telephone from the village. He wondered if it would be all right for him to come up to the house. He has his girlfriend with him.'

'Eh?'

'He wants to speak to you, but I said you were working.' Her eyes took in his slumped form, the tumbler with its half-inch of whisky, the book tented on the floor.

'Pritchard? I don't know any Pritchard. Who is Pritchard?'

'He says he wrote to you. And rang. That you invited him – and his friend.'

'He must be insane.'

'You might have warned me. Anyway, I've told them to come on up. In an hour. We can hardly turn them away – he says they have come all the way from Leeds.'

'Well – who the hell are they? This is intolerable.' Cornelius struggled to his feet, smoothing his disordered hair.

'You had better make yourself respectable for your guests. Where is your other shoe?'

He looked down. He had no idea. He got down awkwardly to look under the sofa. 'This is absurd. Totally absurd. My life seems to be passing into the hands of others.' He had the shoe and sat down to put it on. Bewilderingly, it was another left one, black Oxford instead of brown brogue. 'Dorothy . . .' But Dorothy had left the room.

Outside, it was getting dark already.

'You don't know what it does do to you. You have no idea how much better . . .'

'It would be impossible. Impossible – any of it.' His voice was high-pitched and strained at the end of the argument. 'Can you imagine . . .'

'Be quiet. Listen,' she said. 'There is the bell. They are here. Now, you promised,' she said as she went out into the hall.

It is like the beginning of a play, he thought. There was a discreet babble of voices off. Here came the other players.

Pritchard was exceedingly, disappointingly tall and thin, with a bush of black frizzy hair, a small nose, bright, sly eyes behind blood-red-framed spectacles; a black document-case dangled from one hand, his other foraging forward to grasp Cornelius's.

'Mr Marten. I'm delighted to meet you. Your invitation is a great honour, I need hardly say.'

Cornelius's eyes were on the young woman who had followed Pritchard into the room.

She too was tall and slim. Her hair was very fair, her face a little burned by the sun, her blue eyes looking at the room, at Cornelius, her mouth smiling nervously, her whole face holding a most flattering diffidence. She carried, set down, a large, bulging, brown soft-leather suitcase.

'. . . my letter . . .' said the young man.

Ah, it all dropped suddenly into place. Every now and then Cornelius's mind, too often a jumbled set of tumblers, would click neatly with a sudden, wonderfully satisfying engagement, and his memory would open smoothly. For a moment, or, on a good day, for minutes, he could look inside the safe of the present and see clearly and in a business-like way – then it would be closed to at once, as if a hand had snatched the safe door, slammed it shut, and with a dash of the palm skittered the combination again. He saw the letter in his mind. It had flattered him.

'I am preparing my doctoral thesis on your work, with special reference to the sequence of five novels to which you gave the overall title *The Conquest of Time*. Perhaps you might permit me to call on you the next time I am in London. I would not wish to intrude.' The letter had been addressed care of his publisher, a firm which had undergone several changes of ownership since its old days in Bedford Square, and through which the letter had evidently battled its way over an assault course. The envelope was marked with scribbled pencil comments – Who is this? Do you know where Marten is? Caroline – please ask Julian. And Julian presumably had come up with the answer – the Martens' present address scrawled in red ink. He must have written a reply – that part was clouded. He thought that he remembered a phone call from someone – but had thought it was a repairman of the electrical or gas variety arranging with Dorothy for a visit – 'Yes, yes – you must contact my wife.'

Well, they were here. He had, he believed, behaved most graciously. Settling them down in the drawing-room, directing Dorothy to serve sherry, asking after the severity or otherwise of their journey – he had no idea where Leeds exactly was, he confessed, but had always imagined it as a cold, hard Northern fastness.

It was rather, said Pritchard smiling. And Penny – that was the young woman's name – smiled too, and Cornelius looked at her knees and the thin-bladed bones of her shins and the thin, tapering calves.

Now they sat at the dinner-table. The two men were talking literature. Cornelius heard his own voice making oracular pronouncements that he did not quite understand. He disparaged his contemporaries and praised the long-dead. All through this, Pritchard sat sagely nodding his head in agreement. Then Pritchard was continuing his suddenly boring conversation about his doctoral thesis.

'. . . and I was hoping, over the weekend, if I might record an interview . . .'

The girl really was extremely attractive. Her face in its fine, thin lines, the way that her hand went up to her hair every now and then, transferring the fork to the other hand, to brush back one wing of pale straw – 'the honeyed ramparts at her ear'. What was that line of Yeats? She was not terribly young, not so terribly young. In her mid-twenties, but with an air of innocence and naïvety. As she straightened her back, brushed at her hair again, her face went into the shadow cast by the shade of the low lamp that hung down over the dining-table and Cornelius watched her small breasts rise under her thin sweater and was held by the sight of the unguarded nipples.

'Cornelius – Kevin was saying how much he was looking forward to working with you.' Dorothy's dry voice cut in.

Kevin? Who was Kevin?

'Only that I was so fascinated on reading the novels how your hero negotiates history, how subtly his own predicaments comment ironically on the larger history about him. The subsuming of the individual into the greater . . .'

But, really, now he was glad they had come. He let them gabble on. His irritation had quite disappeared. It was his first good dinner for a long time – he supposed Dorothy must take the credit for that. Two bottles of claret, the second half gone.

He heard the young man say, 'The past.'

'Well, of course, that is quite another matter,' said Cornelius. 'The past. I have been reading much about such things. I wonder if it truly exists. The theories that physicists have now about the fundamental irrationality of time and space. How they are all mixed up. If indeed we do not exist in an innumerable series of parallel worlds. So that you, Helena – ' he said excitedly, looking across the table at Penny, and she looked back at him, and smiled, puzzled, her hair darkening, her mouth growing a little fuller ' – or rather your grandfather or grandmother may walk across a square as children and bump into yourself, a young woman, and you bump shoulders with your own grandson – or rather pass through one another, for there, we assume, can be no contact, for these are all – not ghosts – but inhabitants of the same space at different times. Or you arrive at the same time but in different spaces so that your twenty-year-old grandfather passes, doffing his hat to a lady, his daughter, a charming old lady accompanied by a servant holding a parasol, who is – why, my own wife there. You see – the utter magic of it. All of these seemingly differing generations passing by and through one and another. The true transcendence of time.'

There was silence round the table. He studied the parting in the girl's hair as she bent her head once more. He drained his glass and saw that the second bottle was empty.

'Have we another bottle of this, Dorothy?' he asked. 'I'm sure that our guests would appreciate a little more. I would hate to stint them.'

'No, not for me, please, Mr Marten,' said the young man. 'We drink very little. Not for us.'

The table had miraculously been cleared of dishes. Dorothy was rising.

'You really must be exhausted after your journey,' she said. 'Perhaps I can show you upstairs.'

Did they have two rooms ready for guests? Cornelius wondered. Then he realized with disgust that the wonderful girl was preparing to spend the night with the rather horrible young man, Pritchard. A consolation prize, a large goblet of brandy, appeared in front of him. The young man was leaning forward over the table.

'Until the morning, Mr Marten. You can't know how much I am looking forward to working with you.'

They left him. Time left him. The rose of light the top of the lampshade cast on the ceiling swayed very gently. He heard Dorothy say, 'Good night, Cornelius. Don't stay too long,' but his eyes watched the light, its petals twisting slowly this way and that on the ceiling.

He sipped at his brandy. It was strange to have others in the house. Could he trust the young man? It was so long since anyone had taken an interest in his work. He might be merely one of the many kinds of maniac who infest the literary world. But the girl – ah, the girl was different. He tried to imagine her naked, then felt ashamed of doing so. They must all be asleep. This was how he liked the house, all silent, breathing shallowly in sleep. He looked at the clock on the mantelshelf. To his shock it was not yet ten. Surely they had been gone hours? In answer, there came a dull thud on the ceiling from the room above. A shoe dropping to the floor. They must be in the empty bedroom overhead.

The sound was an intrusion. He would go to the library. Prepare some work for the morning. Prepare for Pritchard. But first he must go to the lavatory.

He came into the hall – occupied by a large, ancient wardrobe, an umbrella stand and a long rectangular cheval glass mounted on castors, facing towards the front door. He came to the foot of the stairs. The house was arranged around a cruciform of the hall, the stairs, and the narrow corridor that ran between drawing-room and kitchen, away like the nave of a church to the library.

He went tipsily up the stairs, holding onto the heavy, gleaming banister. He twisted awkwardly onto the landing. Facing him were the two doors of his bedroom, the bathroom; to his left, at the rear of the house, Dorothy's bedroom; to the right, the nest for the two cuckoos. Trying to be as quiet as possible he entered the bathroom. He peed as noisily as a stallion. Forbore to flush from delicacy. Emerged. Went to the head of the stairs. Then, for some reason, he edged to the door of the guest bedroom. Ah, the reason? He believed he had heard his name whispered. *Marten.*

His hearing was not acute. The door muffled further the man's deep murmurings, the girl's answers that sounded like sighs.

Straining to get as near as he could without actually laying his ear against the panel, he thought he caught his name again. *Marten.*

Then the bed creaked as if one or both of them got in. Silence, that seemed to last and last. His body was growing cold. The black-brown ghost of the door loomed as moonlight shone through the round window, receded as the moon was clouded over. Rain spat on the small, fan-shaped panes. The bed began to creak softly and rhythmically. It seemed to go on and on. He remained, half-crouching at the door. His listened, aware of himself. Why, he asked, cannot an old man stand on his own landing, alone and cold, listening to the sounds of love?

In the morning the country in flood was a dun plain of mirrors and gulls. The birds had flown in from the coast, found calmer water here and stayed.

He saw his guests stroll to the top of the side garden. They stopped at the end copse of birch trees, peered through and turned away. He knew well the dreary view they had just attempted to enjoy. A view of nothing but hedged sheets of water; the grey church tower a mile away, its gilded weathercock rusted in its socket so that it faced permanently away from the wind that blew, hardly deviating, across the flat land from the North Sea.

They came back up the garden. The girl was extraordinary. He took a step back from the window so they would not see him. When they passed through the kitchen, Dorothy would give Pritchard the note saying that Cornelius could see him at eleven.

On the stroke of that hour his guest knocked at the door.

'Come.'

Pritchard had taken off the anorak from his walk. He now wore an olive-green pullover with khaki elbow patches and epaulettes. His thin, unmuscular body looked incongruous in this pseudo-military uniform. For the rest he wore the blue jeans

ubiquitous, if not compulsory, among his generation. A pair of
suede boots with thick yellow soles like slabs of butter completed
the arrangement. He carried the black document case.

'May I . . . ?' He advanced with the tip-toe gait of one
approaching a terminally ill patient in a hospital bed.

'Please.' Cornelius beckoned him to the low chair he had
placed in front of the desk so that he could look down on him.
Pritchard's face was in shadow with his back to the window. He
leaned sideways, unlocking his case. Cornelius switched on the
desk lamp.

'Before you do whatever it is you do,' said Cornelius, 'perhaps
we might have a small preparatory talk. What brings you here?'

'Why, you do, Mr Marten. Mechanically, your call. Spiritually, well, my interest in your work. Your life. You said, for
instance, in *The Conquest of Time* that by the end of his life an
individual should be able to reckon up the responses he has made
to the intellectual commitments of his age, and see if they . . .'

'I no longer think that. You think they make up a man's life?'
said Cornelius. 'Did I say that — "A man's intellecutal
commitments"? – oh no, I do not think for one moment that *they*
are what come up in front of his eyes when he is dying. Do you?
"The intellectual commitments"?'

The young man smiled at him.

'It is not that. Not that,' Cornelius said. 'Do you know what
the four last things are? The last four things we are enjoined to
think of before death?'

'What precisely do you mean?' A canny answer, accompanied
with a wary smile that did not wish to appear entirely ignorant.

'In the Christian catechism they are Death, Judgement,
Heaven and Hell. But in our secular age they should perhaps be
changed. I suggest – First Love, Friendship, Betrayal and Death –

the last is constant. These also happen to be the staples of the novelist. Is that the sort of thing you want?'

'Well . . .' The weasel smile remained, pinned to Pritchard's mouth.

'How do you intend to go about your task? Are you an adept of shorthand?'

Cornelius's right hand trembled, holding pencil over pad in a parody of the interviewing employer.

'I can show you,' said Pritchard, bending and opening his case. 'I brought this down with me.'

A black plastic box appeared on the desk.

'You have no objection? To a tape recorder?'

Cornelius had never used one before. Perhaps if he could not write, he could at least talk.

A button was pressed, a pin-point of red light came on at the end of the box.

'Shall we begin?'

'By all means.'

'In an article you wrote some years ago, you said that you were trying to reclaim the novel for serious political and philosophical expression, indeed that the first and most important influences on your work were the four great British philosophers, Hobbes, Locke, Berkeley and Hume, and their continuing argument about reality. Would you like to tell me a little about your first exposure to them, and how and in what way they did influence your own work?'

And in Cornelius's mind it was as if he had opened a door and stepped from a familiar to an utterly unfamiliar room. He found that he could not remember a single word that any of these four names had ever said or done, or even who they were. The room was full of simpler, infinitely more complicated things.

Every morning my father . . .

The First Thing

Every morning my father, dressed in double-breasted pin-stripe suit and Homburg hat, set off for his jeweller's shop.

Some days, when infant school was on vacation, my mother would take me and follow – two or three hours later – his path. I remember the edge of a cloud emerging from behind a tower whose clock had a face of gold numerals; a spill of oil in a marbled rainbow along the gutter where a blue van had just pulled away. In the street where my father had his shop a hundred impressions are laid each one over the last, as if built up in glass slides, until there is erected a cube in which rain and sunlight fleet after one another, and we arrive at the door. (My eyes even at the age of six were beginning to weaken so that my pre-spectacle images are few, fresh; antediluvian.)

Inside, the shop was sharply modern in the fashion of the twenties. The vast front window had engraved upon it a peacock's open fan which threw a mottled shadow sharply onto the wooden parquet floor under the window, to be lost in the blue, yellow-starred carpet. The chairs for customers were of tubular steel bent into the shape of inverted question marks. The customer's head supplied the dot. My father was usually in the glass office at the rear of the long shop. A pale assistant hurried before to announce our arrival. Father's mouth would be working at the telephone as if it were the ear of a woman. He would look annoyed for a moment, talk a little more into the mouthpiece, replace it on the stand and turn, raising himself in his chair, beaming and saying something I cannot hear.

I begin to run across the shop floor to him. He comes smiling from the office and I cling to his legs until he swings me up and my face is at the level of his and I smell his shaving lotion and run my fingers in and along the round, hard pink furrows of his brow as he smiles.

Set down again; my mother talks over my head for a few minutes. Then we leave the shop and resume our walk, calling at the dressmaker's, the lending library – perhaps one of my mother's friends for lunch. Once we were stopped in the street by a man. I studied the cross-checks of his trousers while my mother talked in a low voice, turning a little away from me. Before we walked off he kissed her hand. Then we went home and Mother sat down to write a letter, shooing me away.

We had a maid and a cook. The maid was a tall, religious girl with one eye that looked in a different direction from the other. When she twisted my ears or pulled at my hair as she washed me, one eye would be cocked to Heaven, watching for a signal that her good work was being noticed.

Cook had huge upper arms of blue-veined alabaster, red, wrinkled elbows and tiny, quick hands.

A house of women. I longed for the time when Father came home. After dinner he sat at the opened bureau in the corner of the sitting-room sorting stones under the green-shaded lamp.

One night he leans down to where I lie with a book on the carpet. 'Look, Cornelius. Look at this. Look through it at the fire.' I take the red stone; its thin side-facets meet in pyramids at each end. I hold it to my eye. The room tilts and divides into a steeply angled crystal cavern full of tiny paintings on its six walls. Our white terrier, Polly, is multiplied, her faces absurdly small and sharp within the stone, her pink tongues, as she pants by the fire, tiny red, trembling jewels.

'Now, isn't that beautiful?' says my father. It is. I look down at it in my cupped palm, bewitched by this token of love. 'Keep it.'

I take it to school the next day and whisper to my friend Rinus that I have a great treasure. He begs me to show it him. Reluctantly I hand on the stone under the desk. Seven boys along each long form. We wear shorts and the front edge of the form presses into the backs of our legs. When a boy stands you can see white-red ledges in the flesh. Now Rinus is looking at the stone. Before I can stop them the boy next along takes it off Rinus. It begins to be passed hand to hand. The stone crosses the aisle and proceeds along the next bench – heads bent and raised again as it is examined. Passed forward – about to cross the divide again – when the master brings down his pointer with a *thwack* on the front desk.

The boy in possession has to show what is in his hand. The master takes the stone and holds it up to the window. It is clear that he had not expected this. He turns it one way, another. 'Well – what of it?' he demands.

'It's a jewel, sir,' a boy calls out.

'A jewel? Nonsense.' The master holds the stone aloft again, peering through. 'This is merely a piece of glass. What is there so interesting about a piece of glass?'

All morning the stone sat on his desk. At break, after gathering his papers, he tossed it contemptuously into the waste-paper basket behind him. I had not the heart to retrieve it.

An intense Anglophile, my father dipped Bath Olivers into Earl Grey tea while reading the *Continental Daily Mail*. He made frequent business trips to England in the late twenties and early thirties, bringing back scarlet-tunniced lead soldiers for me and news of the latest musical shows for Mother.

He admired all things English. In particular their habit of sending young males away to boarding-school. This was the Secret of Their Success; the foundation of their Empire. His son must be made privy to the secrets of that army of administrators and traders who had made half the world their warehouse.

He would have sent me to school in England, but my mother prevented him. It was not until I was twelve that he found a suitable establishment. And actually run by an Englishman.

Well, a Scotsman, but the next best thing, I suppose.

Murray's Academy. A few miles outside the capital. The day of the Interview.

My father left his shiny black saloon under a wet, disconsolate-looking pine tree. I waited, my bowels liquefying, on the gravel at the foot of grey stone steps. My father knocked loudly and confidently on the double oak doors. One opened a crack. He leaned forward and spoke to the crack. Removing his hat, beckoning me up the steps, he entered; I followed.

Red and black chequered floor. Dark panelling. A huge, dimpled gong. A maid going before us, youngish, with thick ankles in grey stockings. No sound of boys. No smell of ink and chalk. Another oak door, awesome in shadowed silence.

The maid knocked, waited for what must have been a telepathic signal, and timorously ushered us in.

'The Martens,' she announced, and dissolved back into darkness.

My father guided me in. Something impersonating light fell in a mournful shaft from an improbably tall, draped window. The dimness caught a long, narrow, bald head and pince-nez so highly polished that even in the gloom they shone wickedly. The face was not so much thin as composed of deep vertical folds, as if deflated from a former fullness. The white, black-haired hands that searched among his papers were powerful. They gave up the search. He looked up.

'Aye so, Marten – this is the boy?'

'My son,' said Father, with some pride.

'And what is your name?' Shining, eyeless lenses fixed on me.

'Cornelius,' I stammered.

The haggard god sniffed.

'. . . sir.'

'My name is Murray. Doctor Murray. Are you happy to continue this conversation in English – or your own tongue?'

'Cornelius has learned English since age four,' said my father. Murray ignored him.

I don't remember much of what was directed at me. He did ask one of those fiendishly phrased arithmetical riddles: those things about six and a half men sawing down two and two-thirds hectares of trees in one hour twenty minutes, so how long would it take one man? Or one man fills sixty baths in a hotel, another man . . . My mind froze. The lunatics ran from room to room. The water flowed. This man waited on his answer.

My father broke in: 'Can't you see the boy is terrified?' I was ashamed. Why did he have to say that? 'He has a good enough head for figures.'

'Well, well – it hardly matters,' said Murray, suddenly genial. 'Only to see if we have another Newton on our hands. Now as to the matter of fees . . .'

When we came out, my father halted by the car and looked back at the deep-red brick walls, the fantastically gabled roofs.

'Ah,' he sighed. 'It is what I have always wanted for you, Cornelius.'

I found out later that the building had first served as a hospital for the victims of venereal disease. Later, as if by a natural progression, it had been an orphanage for children of the fleeting alliances made between the military personnel of various nations and the women of our small country. When I arrived there a month after the interview, the building seemed smaller. The dowdy shrubs that surrounded the large front lawn presumably flowered in the vacations – I never saw them do so.

From my lovely, ship-in-bottled room at home I here ascended each night to a dormitory where twenty other boys undressed, folded their clothes and hung them in upright lockers like coffins. Mistrustful, searching for alliances, we stowed towels and toothbrushes in the tiny bedside cupboards bequeathed to us by the syphilitics and military bastards.

One morning all the other boys had risen and gone and I was left sick in my bed. It was my second-year. The sun slanted in. At the top of the dormitory was a black iron stove that warmed only that end. I shivered under the sheet and two thin blankets.

The pale sunlight showed our young dust floating, and imprinted the window-frames on the wall opposite; they moved and bloomed and paled all morning until someone came to look for me.

Influenza. I did not tell the doctor who came to the school sick-bay about the nights I had stood in front of the half-open dormitory window, barefoot, cradling cold in my arms, watching the closed school gates against the night sky. Unless I shouted it in my fever. My parents came and sympathized and left. Six whole weeks had passed when at last I started to recover. I had missed the spring vacation, but grown content with my lazing life. With the weather warming I was allowed to sit in the glass conservatory at the side of the sick-bay. Facing south, it was grandly called the Solarium. There was a huddle of pot plants on the brick floor, an ancient leather couch, and a row of sunned books on the window ledge. The only English book was a fat little blue-cloth *Palgrave's Golden Treasury*. I stretched out on the couch. Poetry. There was nothing else to read. I opened it at the back. *Clouds*. Rupert Brooke. 'Down the blue night the unending columns press . . .'

And, above, through the glass roof, though it was day, the

clouds did just that. It was as if an electric current had passed up my arms from the book, sparking in my brain. If you read the poem now it seems ordinary enough for its time – but I cannot renege on the effect it had on me then. The clouds pressing over the conservatory, the lines of verse, my late fever. At once I knew what I must be. A poet. I devoured the poem again and again. I suffered a lesser but still potent intoxication from others in the book. Swinburne, Francis Thompson, Rossetti – it is not the greatest literature that seduces us. There is nothing later to equal this first meeting with cunningly arranged words.

A poet? The dose of ridicule I got when I returned to the dormitory resolved me to keep quiet about my new passion. The world was not greatly interested in what went on in my skull. And the world had changed.

At night, pastimes were different. At the far end of the dormitory a party of boys, with the help of a candle, vied with each other to throw the biggest possible shadows of their newly-sprouted prongs on the wall.

I was quite amazingly puritanical about such things, but soon – like all the others – I lived in a state of almost constant sexual excitation. The school was a heaving prison, with each of us in a blood-coloured cell, while masters patrolled the corridors, flicking back the Judas eyes to try and catch us at our mucky outrages.

I do not think any of this engendered homosexual feelings in me. The communal pleasures had, of course, reached with some boys a more active stage than mere comparison. I began to understand why boys fainted at morning prayers.

I knew nothing of women, of course. At home, an only child, without a revelatory brother or sister, my female cousins moved above and below me in scornful orbits.

Enough of school.

I am seventeen. I am home for Christmas. Next year I shall prepare for the University. After dinner with my mother and father in which I hear nothing that they say, I hurry away to look out from the second-floor landing window at the front of the house.

The gables opposite are loaded with fresh snow that has fallen heavily and that is still falling thinly. On the road below are the firmly braided, intertwined tracks of only two, three cars that have passed. All is silent and still. I open the window and let the cold air thrill me. At last I let the lace half-curtain fall back into place. I make my way through the wandering corridor to my bedroom at the back. From the window there I see the moon silver the paved courtyard. The snow has fallen only to one side of the narrow well. On our pale-grey statue of stooping Atalanta and her two silver-gilt apples, where the thin facing has dropped away, are islands and archipelagos of black, pitted stone.

I turn back to the room; the maid has not been up and my bed is still disordered from the morning. The first two lines of real poetry enter my heart and come from my tongue.

> In winter one white sheet
> lies on the floor and the luminous city . . .

The first gesture, reflex, of a frozen mind waking. The lines are in English. My own language is, as someone said, fit only for horses. I am going to be a great English poet.

I sleep easily that night, in the innocent, unanxious sleep still available on the edges of childhood. I wake late. Father is at the shop. Mother has gone out to a friend. Neither has left any instructions as to how I am to spend the day. For the first time I can please myself.

I go for a walk.

I am standing in the middle of a flat land, on the eastern edge of the red and white small capital of that land. I feel superbly elated. There is nothing in my head really but the intellectual garbage of any other seventeen-year-old, but yet such an excitement in me. I assemble the elements of my genius: I stand on earth; I am on fire; I look between the bared trees at the iced water of the lake; I draw into my lungs the diamond air.

Behind me the Museum assembles its own superior, equal, and inferior elements. I turn and walk towards the yellow-white portico and mount the wide steps. The young man who walks up the steps is slight, yet with overall something springy in his whole aspect, from the balls of his feet to the upward-jutting quiff of black hair; his lips are slightly parted, showing small, white, almost childlike teeth; his eyes are expectant behind the wire-framed spectacles.

In the great hall the electric lamps are soft and yellow. On the staircase, where natural light comes through tall windows, the filaments glow feebly.

The first gallery has huge portraits of my father's business friends in seventeenth-century fancy dress. Only – they should have cigarettes in their hands, and the blackamoor boy hold a cocktail shaker instead of a pineapple.

My shoes sound loud on the wooden-tiled floor. The place is empty except for an attendant who picks morosely at the thick rope that loops from one chromed column to the next. I don't want to see him.

Next is a narrow, long room, with doors at each corner. At the end almost the whole wall is taken up by a large painting. A bull stands beside a tawny-bodied, white-faced cow, who is lying down. There is a lake, reflecting blue sky, small white clouds, behind the beasts. A pollarded tree leans across the edge of the lake, and a bearded, straw-hatted cowman leans against the tree. But the subject of the painting is the bull.

He looks like one of those illustrations in a cookbook, wanting only numbers enclosed in little balloons floating on strings from his body to demonstrate the cuts. The bull peers endlessly and blindly to the other end of the room, to another herd of cows – again under trees, this time in charge of a man who is playing some distant, farting cousin of the recorder. Two small children, wrapped in a ball, wrestle. A view of water, horned and tailed. A distant tower. The same high, pale, blue sky.

And here, wandering through the far left door, comes a girl. She stands for a moment looking up at the bull. Wavy black hair curls over her thin shoulders. She has on a simple black dress drawn in at the waist with a dark-blue belt. It falls to just below the knee and her legs are very slender. I pretend to look at a small landscape: trees, water, spire. She walks on through the other door. But first she has looked round and I have seen her face. The skin is very white, the eyes large and brown, her red lips appearing slightly swollen. Over one arm she carries a navy-blue outer coat with a brown fur collar. I have no choice but to follow her.

The next room is small, square, window drapes drawn to, the air thick with yellow light. Here is the painting I have come to see. Rembrandt's *The Anatomy Lesson of Professor Culp*; on loan to our city. I stand by her side. Well, an arm's length from her side, my heart bumping.

We both look at the picture. The surgeon, his face full of a pale gentleness, lifts the flayed arm, displaying the exposed tendons; while the fearful, inquiring faces of his students with their long noses peer at the open book of anatomy, at Culp's hand, into space – anywhere but at the bulky-chested, livid corpse that lies foreshortened on the dissecting table.

After a moment or two she moves. I follow her out of the corner of my eye. She pauses in front of the picture on the adjoining wall. Interior: a kitchen. A woman bears a basket of clothes across the chocolate-brown and yellow-white chequered floor to the door that opens on the sunlit yard. *The*, not *a* — specificity is the secret of art, not generalization.

As the girl leans forward to look closer at the picture, I cross again, closer to her. And what enters my mind is — should I lean down beside her, pretending to be interested in the same bottom section of the same small picture? I am only a foot away from her. I fancy I can hear her breathing.

Then she straightens up and looks at me. Her eyes, deep sherry-brown, regard me with candour and amusement. The black hair curls naturally on her white brow and waves to her shoulders. A tall, slim adolescent I had reckoned her to be from a distance. Now I see she is older than I am. Eighteen? Nineteen? She smiles.

'It's much the best, isn't it?' she says, entering my future. My past . . . 'It's so personal. So alive.' She reached out her hand. The fingertips, with nails like pearls, touched the side of the frame and travelled slowly and lovingly down. 'I should love this for my room.'

And of course I thought that then she would make some trite comment about the Rembrandt, though marvellous, being a little overpowering for the room — or some such nonsense. But she left it at that. Or rather, not at that.

'Do you mind if I go round with you? You are on your own?' she asked.

I stood irresolutely. Answering her own question, she took a step forward and linked her arm in mine. 'We might just as well,' she said. 'We seem to be the only ones here.'

I can't remember what we talked about. That tortures me. I

should remember every word. But somehow she was my due that day, what I deserved for becoming a poet; my first Muse. So we talked of Art and Life; Politics; the Death of God; Jazz; the Movies. I discovered that the film I had seen on a day of the previous week she had watched at the very same time, at the back of the cinema while I sat at the front, the same Gary Cooper chiaroscurating over our far-apart faces. She thought him very beautiful. I, reluctantly, agreed. We came too quickly to the last room in the gallery.

At the foot of the steps outside she said she must go the opposite way to me. She had to be back at six, this being Christmas Eve. It was with such charming regret that she said this. She stood and looked at me. I realized that she expected me to say something in return. Before I could stammer out, 'Goodbye then,' which was all my miserable mind could come up with, she said, with a sort of puzzled amusement, 'We shall meet again? It was nice.'

'Yes. Yes – of course.'

'Well then, you must choose. You're the man.' She held her fur collar to her throat and pretended or did not pretend to shiver with cold.

It had got dark. There were lights among the trees on the far side of the lake.

We fixed to meet in a café in town three days after the holiday. No, she couldn't get away sooner. It didn't occur to me to ask where she lived. I had to be at home over Christmas, I said. She did too.

So we parted for the first time and I watched her walk quickly away along the front of the Museum on the gravel path until she was nothing but a wraith at the end of the colonnaded front. A fool, I started to walk the other way, and only checked myself in time to see her halt at the corner and lift her hand and wave to me.

In my bedroom I flew to the piece of paper on which I had written those two lines the night before. I wrote a deal more that night that was addressed now not to myself, but to . . . I did not even know her name. But it is all sex, is it not? All creative energy is sexual in origin. When a man gets old and impotent, it is not only his cock that has withered and hidden itself away – it is his pride, his wit, his ability to create.

I must have written a hundred lines, each worse than the last, until I slumped down on my bed in the small hours. I woke to the zinc dazzle of Christmas morning.

The house was suddenly full. Of people whose arrival the night before I had not seen, stuck scribbling away in my room. Now, as I came down into the house, they unfurled their slumberous forms, their heavy, unlovely shapelessnesses, and crossed and re-crossed the landing in dressing gowns, uncollared shirts, unpetticoated skirts; fragments of night and day attire curiously mixed. They waited, unwashed, smelling of the complications of adult sleep, babbling by the frosted-glass-paned, steamed-up bathroom door like a line of rich refugees, waiting for the washed, the blessed, the perfumed, the glistening, new-shaven, alcohol-rubbed, hair strands blackened by water over bald pates, or frosted blonde frizzes, the sexes intermingled, beaming and greeting from watery resurrection. O worthy, wordy, over-worded people. Not their words. Mine. Too many. I fled back to my room. Crept down again, an hour later, to the dripping bathroom, wraithed with ghosts of steam, littered with the fallen bodies of sodden blue and white and red and white and jazz-striped towels, slaughtered on the floor, or hanging out of the bath like so many assassinated Marats.

The house had absorbed them, dried them. I came down the stairs, superior, in love with youth, with myself, with my girl.

'Come now, Cornelius – where have you been?' said my mother, meeting me on the stair. She took me to meet more newly arrived visitors in the hallway. The men were polar bears in huge white overcoats, the women snouted beavers or sleek-rumped otters.

They kissed me. They all had moustaches; the men and the women. I did not kiss them. They swept past me.

In the drawing-room, its doors opened to the dining-room, they met, like a tide, the beaming beach of last night's residents.

Each to each, they proffered presents, accepted drinks. They whooped. Faces grew red. I stood by the door. A bad mistake, as I became the first greeter of newcomers. Some of them knew me. The hall became an emporium of coats, hanging in mounds on tottering hall-stands. The floor of the dining-room became a counter of ripped and abandoned pink and blue and gold-striped paper, empty rectangles and lozenges of string.

And through them all, through the rooting Christmas dinner, with its facing rows of braying, soughing, whinnying and shouting Gogolian, Hogarthian, Grosz-esque faces and hands and smeared napkins and bones in grease-runnelled knuckles, moved the ghost of my slender Beatrice. I did not even know her name.

The two days of Christmas went like an unbelievably slow funeral past me.

At last the compulsory familial conviviality was at an end. The guests prepared to depart. Those who disliked each other travelled away in taxis to the station, chattering eagerly and maliciously about those left behind.

Why do I wish them always to be seen in a bad light? The poor dears are dead, long dead. Their graves are neglected – if they had them. If my words are their only memorials then I am sorry for that.

After the two days of the holiday my father reopened his shop in town, and fled to it with protestations of regret, and joy in his face.

I could at last go out. To meet my . . . My what? Putative mistress? My hands sweated dreadfully, even in the cold as I hurried along. I rubbed them in the pockets of my greatcoat.

She was waiting outside the café. She had on the same winter coat, held with one hand at the collar against the cold. To my delight, she was as beautiful as I had remembered and endlessly imagined. We shook hands. I worried how mine felt.

I held the door open.

An elaborately ornate cornucopia of flowers and fruit was engraved on the glass panel, partly obscured by a garishly Expressionist poster advertising an exhibition of work by artists who had fled from Germany. The place had been redecorated by one of those couples who dabble in the arts when young, fail, and take to cookery. They had failed at this also and now the place was let to a middle-aged German who was writing, or endlessly threatening to write, a satirical novel about the small colony of bohemians in our respectable city. They patronized the café in order not to be excluded. At any rate, he was not much seen and dispensed his coffee and delicious Viennese pastries through the proxies of his wife and her mother, and an elderly male whose connection with the family was undefined. This man, like the unfortunate professor in *The Blue Angel*, combined exquisitely refined manners and excessive erudition with the comically reduced position of having to sweep the floors and clear and wipe tables. Perhaps, after they had closed, late at night he would prance and cluck like a chicken, while the owner's mother-in-law straddled with mottled thighs a chair in front of the counter, a cigarette dangling negligently from her fingers, a top hat tipped back on her head.

All of this, some invented, all – I imagined – witty, I told to Helena as we sat at a table waiting to be served.

The truth was that I had only been in the place once before.

Helena gently corrected me.

The German was not writing a novel; he had written a similar one a few years before, though. He was ill upstairs. The old man was a great-uncle, who had been *maître d'hôtel* before the Nazis had forced the family from Berlin. And all this was said so mildly, after she had smiled at each of my inventions, not as if she were really correcting me, but adding to my jokes. She knew this place.

'I suppose they are Jews then?' I said.

'Yes, they are. What of it.'

Her eyes rested levelly and placidly in mine.

'Oh. I didn't mean. I'm sorry. I mean . . .' I didn't mention my mother's side of the family.

The coffee had arrived. It was plain that I had to take a step up into the adult world. At seventeen, indeed, the whole world appears an ascending staircase, its walls littered with confusing signs. Say this, not that. Do this, not that. Appear grown-up. Do not be childish . . . Thank God we're not there forever.

I said the only sensible thing I have ever said: 'I am absurd. Can we start this conversation again? How long have you been in the city?'

Two years. She had come from just over the border. No, she had no parents. She would prefer not to talk about it. No, nothing had happened to them. She had been brought up by an aunt. It was as much to escape from her aunt as anything else that she had crossed over. What about you?

I was a poet. Not a schoolboy. I said neither. What then did we talk about?

Again, the movies, music, the paintings we had seen. I found to my surprise that she knew well books I thought were my private discoveries: Joyce, Alain-Fournier, Rimbaud. She had lived in Paris for a year.

'So I know those things, you see,' she said modestly.

My world seemed to have shrunk to this café, this table – her. The money for this outing had been stolen from Father's cash box; I had also decanted a quarter of a pint of brandy into a medicine bottle. To give me courage.

It was late afternoon when we came out. Already the sun was gone, only its ice-green afterlight clinging to top-storey windows of the terraced apartments across the street.

'We could go to the cinema,' she suggested as I stood, once more uncertainly, on the pavement. As we walked to The Rialto, I fingered the bottle in my pocket.

Directed sideways by the eccentric moon of the usherette's torch, we sat in an empty row. The great curved auditorium held perhaps thirty or forty people this afternoon; the usual freight of lovers, tramps, and lonely paederasts, whose eyes ignored the screen, instead roaming sadly across the empty spaces in search of truant schoolboys. A thick veil of grey-blue cigarette smoke drifted down the long pyramid of light. At its base, a couple in evening dress swirled on the screen. Thin, puritanically abandoned Mr Astaire; Ginger of the slim, practised sensuality. Her eyes were extraordinary.

Then – ? Backstage a man in a booth and moustache talks energetically into a telephone. We cannot hear him for the music. Ah – a break for the young dancers. A misunderstanding. An argument based on that. A tiff. Girl, Ginger, walks out on partner, Fred, to team up with moustache. Hugely successful. Fred dancing alone. Moustache and Ginger whirling faster and faster. Not really happy. Tour. A train thunders through a blizzard of ghostly calendar leaves. 2nd Jan. 3rd March. Train bursts through successive hoops of theatre posters, flat forest of

station names: Atlantic City; Topeka; Denver; Chicago –
onwards, onwards the great steam engine thrusts its phallically
veined and piped boiler, as the past – dates, towns, posters –
rushes at breakneck speed away. Until . . . New York!

I had no interest in the damn thing. I could not recognize
beauty except by my side. Her face, made luminous in the light
from the screen, breathed in the grey lovers' breath, laughed at
their mock misunderstandings and at the comic butler and the
idiotic Italian count. Then she saw me watching her and smiled,
turning her body in the seat lightly towards me. I bent my head. I
shall – I can now with not the slightest difficulty – recover that
first kiss forever. The building, the city, the absurdity of myself
swayed away, as if deflected forever into space by some infinitely
benign and sweet Angel who would forever intervene at every
moment of my life, to press my lips and forever extinguish the
horrible tyranny of I. The only purely ecstatic moment of my life.
The sort on which religions are founded. If they were not founded
by half-starved hermits in torment and caves. And yet, as we
parted, and I kissed her a second time (I must, mustn't I?), I felt
horribly knowing, so that the experience was already curiously
flattened and compromised by my knowledge. Sweetness of
sweetness still – but known now.

The film ended. Because we had come in after the beginning,
we sat on, as the lights dawned up in their green and orange fans
around the walls. We held hands. The house filled more for the
second show. We watched the first film. The B. I cannot
remember that. Then a cartoon of black and white animals. The
second film. The musical. At the exact point where we had come
in, her hand squeezed mine and we rose and shuffled past the
averted knees of the newcomers.

We came out into the night. We still held hands. This, I knew,
was love. The stuff of all literature and poetry and art – though all

that seemed now merely a decoration invented by cynics to obscure the real, the actual thing.

'*Kennst du das Land, wo die Zitronen blühn?*' I recited, flinging my arm up dramatically to indicate the street lights. Comparing them to . . . lemons?

'Come on,' she said, laughing.

Why can one no longer write of love?

Why can no one write of love?

We walked through the city. Along the main streets, which are not so wide, being bordered everywhere, it seems, by water, canals, lakes, stagnant little pools behind closed lock gates, or hemmed in by the ancient houses leaning towards one another overhead, the proud, complacent architecture of the last century, the shipping offices and apartments, and brokers' houses and shops with their long new windows, the mannequins lit and posturing to each other – until we came to an archway.

She pointed to a house in the square through the arch. All the houses were broad, double-faced, four or five storeys high in a continuous squared terrace so that their roofs and chimneys wandered up and down in a polite, solid, prosperous rhythm against the blue night. I stood in the square. At first I did not understand what she was asking me.

'You will come in for a minute or so?' she said. 'There's no need to be worried. There will be no one at home.'

We walked across to what seemed to be the tallest, the broadest keystone residence of the whole square.

'The house is shut for the winter.' She inserted a key in the front door. 'They are all in South Africa. There's only the housekeeper here. Sh . . .'

We tip-toed inside.

She shut the door. We were in utter darkness. Then she turned on a switch. An electric chandelier lit the hall. It was the base of a deep well. Double doors on each side, and twin staircases ascending to a landing and a railed gallery. A wood-tiled, thick-rugged floor. In the centre a tall coat-stand, bare like a tree. On one wall, a large dark oil of a bulging-waistcoated and potato-faced man. All dark woods, colonial woods, the panelling round the hall and up the stairs. Helena – did I forget to tell you her name? – stood by a large panel of switches. She turned off the chandelier. One side only of one staircase was now lit by an ascending curved diagonal of green-shaded lamps. The white-faced man grew very dark and lonely. She turned on two other switches. She took my hand and led me up the staircase.

The landing had another array of heavy doors, single this time. Along the gallery, a short corridor. Another staircase, thinner-carpeted, to another landing, stretching away, more doors, and smaller, meaner, darker pictures. The lights were now dim, in heavy glass ceiling roses. Another flight of stairs, lit by one moon-shaped-shaded bulb at the top. Now there were no pictures, only wallpaper embossed with dull gold on cream with heraldic roses, and only three doors, in a row, corresponding, I thought, to the gables at the top of the house. We went past the first two; one panelled with a glass fanlight above it, cocked half-open, the next solid and threatening. 'The housekeeper . . .' Helena whispered. The next, a few feet on, was its twin; heavy, four-panelled, brass-knobbed. Beside it, another bank of yellow-white bakelite switches mounted on an oak board. Helena switched three of them and we were plunged once again into absolute blackness.

'This,' she whispered, but now I thought to create an atmosphere of mystery rather than to be quiet, 'is my room.'

She was used to the dark. I heard the door open. Then we were in a room with its curtains open so that the glow from the street lamp far beneath shone in. 'Shut the door,' she whispered. She turned on the light.

We stood on boards of honey-coloured wood. It was the same wood, cut into the same long planks, though not sea-stained, of the captain's cabin of a barque that my father had sometimes taken me onto as a boy when he had business to conduct in port.

A thin, worn, circular rug worked in scarlet and green and blue with birds and trees lay at the side of a plain pine table and two straight-backed chairs; another, large, dark red, rectangular rug was in front of a small gas fire; a sagging armchair. The bed. I had not expected the bed. A brass bedstead; only a white bottom sheet, two pillows, one on top of the other. The window was in a gable with a deep sill that held a leaning row of books. She crossed to the window and began to draw the curtains.

'No – please don't,' I said.

She stared back in surprise.

'It's, it's such a marvellous night. Leave them. No one can see in. I like to look at the night.'

'And me.' She left the curtains half-open. 'Please, sit down.'

A small bookcase with a pile of illustrated magazines on top. One of those Murillo-esque oleographs of a peasant girl on the wall above. A huge wardrobe. Its long, narrow door-mirror encased a section of the bed.

There was a low *plumpft* as she lit the gas fire.

'It is cold,' I said redundantly.

'I'm sorry. Would you like something? Coffee? Soup? I can easily get it.'

'Down all those stairs? It's not necessary. Really.'

'No – I have a gas ring here.'

She squatted by the fire, shedding her coat.

'Take yours off,' she said. 'It will soon be warm.'

I laid my coat over the back of the armchair and took the bottle from the pocket. 'I've got some cognac here.' I felt greatly daring.

'How marvellous.' She got up and went across to the small wash-basin in the corner by the window. She washed out two glasses.

I poured a half-inch into each. She sat on the rug in front of the fire. She set the drink down carefully by her hip and eased off her shoes.

I sat rather prissily on the edge of the armchair. The room was still cold. Her arms around her knees, the black skirt pulled tight as a tent, she gazed down at the rug. Her mouth was open a little, showing small white teeth. She looked up at me. There seemed a complete trust and acceptance in her eyes. Why do I say that – seemed? There was complete trust, acceptance. Leaning forward, falling forward on my knees to the rug, I melted to her. We kissed. I moved her glass. I sat beside her, my arm round her thin shoulders. A man, a fool, I reached for my glass from the chair's arm and drank it down. We kissed again and whispered, and kissed and whispered in each other's arms, for a long time. I wanted nothing else.

Then she said, 'Please – would you turn on that lamp in the corner behind us and turn the main light off? It's so bright it makes me cold.'

When I came back, she was lying in front of the fire, her hands at the back of her head, her knees drawn up, the yellow glow of the fire on one side of her face, the other in my shadow.

'Take your jacket off,' she said. All this time, the earnest, bespectacled student had been encased in his thick tweed jacket.

I obeyed, but this time stupidly sat down again on the edge of the armchair. I poured some more cognac for myself. Now suddenly the room was very quiet, with only the inconstant shush-shushing sound of the gas fire's jets. Between the curtains I could see the blue-black night surrounding a grey, snow-capped gable across the square. I sipped, in what I hoped was a satisfactorily sophisticated manner, at my drink.

'What are you thinking about?' she asked softly.

She raised herself on one elbow, looking towards the window to see what I found so interesting.

Something, I supposed, after another two minutes' soulful, profile-turned, inconclusive meditation, would have to be done. I slid from the chair. Resting on my knees, I looked down at her. Now she lay on her back, her eyes closed, her face totally composed. Had she fallen asleep? Surely the drink had not made her unconscious so soon? She breathed in slowly and regularly and her small bosom rose and fell. I slumped back against the chair. She had drawn one leg up a little further – I stared in disbelief and wonder. I was a voyeur all at once translated into the world of his keyhole-shaped dreams. Her skirt had fallen back and just above the cream-coloured stocking top was the white of her thigh, and a glimpse of saffron-coloured underwear. I could – can – think of no words to describe my feelings – a sort of tumultuous, excited fear . . . I put out a tentative hand. Withdrew it. Looked at her face. It seemed set in a dream. Was this a test? If so, had I passed some kind of chaste challenge – or failed pitifully?

I remained in this awkward, absurd position for what seemed long, long minutes. Then, convinced by now that she must be asleep, I sat back in the chair and watched over her, drinking slowly the last of the brandy. I had not even the consolation of feeling drunk. It must be that she slept – that marvellous placidity of expression and that tiny bubble of crystal-clear saliva between her lips were surely unfakable, the genuine tokens of innocent, unassailably chaste sleep. So I sat and drank. At last – after a good half-hour, it seemed – she stirred and opened her eyes. She smiled as if she had come from some inexpressibly delightful dream.

'I shouldn't drink. I'm sorry,' she murmured.

'No, no,' I protested.

She jumped up, smacking at her skirt with her hands to smooth it out. She was very awake now. 'Would you like some soup? You must be hungry?'

'No. Really . . .'

'I will make some soup.' She had decided for me. 'It only needs warming.'

The gas ring, a yellow-enamelled saucepan on it, was on the side of the sink. What a strange life it must be for Helena, I thought, to live here with no one for company but the grim housekeeper. And where was she? Asleep? Moving about the house? Perhaps Helena had made her up, as a possible imaginary ally she could threaten me with if I . . . I began to wonder if Helena was indeed quite alone in this huge house, a marvellous, fairy-tale creature who had no real connection with this or any other place, but had merely settled here like a bird when the house was closed for the winter.

She brought me a bowl filled with a clear soup the amber colour and transparency of Pears' Soap.

As I drank it, she went over to a chest at the foot of the bed and took out two blankets and a sheet and began to make up the bed. When she had straightened the top blanket she came and knelt by the fire.

Now, this is important. For arrant, huge stupidity.

Ah, she wants to go to bed, I thought. 'What time is it?' I asked.

'Ummm . . . ? Sorry, my watch has stopped. Ten. Half-past perhaps.'

Ten! What would my father say? My mother? When I had been expected back at five for tea. When we dined at eight.

'I'm sorry, I'm late. I didn't mean to stay so long. And I can see you want to go to bed. I must really go home.'

She looked at me, puzzled. I was putting on my jacket, picking up my overcoat. We went down the stairs in darkness; she tiptoeing in front, holding my hand against the small of her back. In the hallway the fanlight above the door showed twenty to eleven on the coffin-shaped clock. Mirrored in its glass my face was greywhite.

'You don't have to go.'

I kissed her, feeling immensely splendid – the lover tearing himself away. She opened the front door and I slipped out.

'One moment.' Her call followed me down the few shallow steps. She came out and down the steps. She took my hand and pressed a tiny slip of paper into it. 'You forgot this.'

'What is it?'

'The telephone number,' she said, laughing. Then she ran back up the stairs into the house. She blew me a kiss from the opening. The door closed.

The sky was sharply starred. I walked through a still city. Occasionally a car passed demurely, as if afraid to wake me out of my trance, down the centre of a strange, snowy street. The small, companionable city huddled around me, like a, like a . . .

What is this desire to compare everything with something else? Nothing is like anything else. But we live in metaphors and similes, we literary gents. Even when I had been in Helena's room I had been studying my own behaviour. My curiosity was at its most intense when we were most intimate. Even when, in kissing her, I should have been most sublimely unaware, my right eye, my left obscured by the sweep of her fragrant hair, had opened to watch her soft, closed eyes, lashes, her intensity.

But there was none of this as I walked. All my senses were doubly alive. I experienced, ridiculously late, in those cold, clear streets, the urgent sexual arousal I should have felt hours before. I limped home.

In the morning I ate breakfast with Father and Mother and wondered what on earth I had in common with them. I, who at the age of seventeen had spent the night – well, almost spent, almost the night – with a girl. A woman.

They questioned me gently enough. Curtly, I told them that I had run into a schoolfriend. We had gone to the movies, then back to his parents' house. My father became annoyed at my surly answers and said angrily, 'Well, if your friends are to leave you in this mood I am sorry I ever sent you to that school. It is supposed to present gentlemen to the world. Evidently it has not had the desired effect.'

None of this mattered. I sat there with down-turned mouth, moodily scoring the thick white table-cloth with my knife. Instead of perceiving myself as his child any more, I knew that I was now a lover, a poet – almost a man. Not among men, perhaps . . .

But when I stole into the sitting-room a little later in the morning – Father had gone to his office – my hand hesitated over the telephone. What horrors had I committed last night? Did Helena think I was a drunk – a tipsy little delinquent? (I had stowed the empty bottle between the two mattresses on my bed.) Had I behaved as a gentleman? A proper man? An improper man? A properly improper man? Had I been too forward? Backward? Oh God, yes, that was it. But the alternative seemed impossible. She had given me the telephone number – did she intend me to ring it? Perhaps it was just one of the conveniences of polite courtship that she felt obliged to maintain? I assumed at once, you see, that, although totally innocent, she must know of all the alternatives – all of the things my filthy, loving imagination had conjured up about her that would have been unutterably vile to her mind. No. She had made that special trip out into the square to give me the slip of paper. No. She must like me. Yes. I picked up the telephone, dialled her number and, just as it began to ring at the other end, dropped the receiver back on its cradle.

It would be easier, fairer, I thought, to let her get back to normal. To leave her for a couple of days to think about the implications of our affair for the future . . .

Half an hour later I re-enacted the pantomime. This time I hung on as the other end rang and rang. At last someone answered. Although she sounded different I knew it was her.

'Is that you?' I whispered.

'Hello – is there anybody there?' she said brightly.

Too much whisper. 'Hu . . . Hullo,' I stuttered, my breath hardly reaching into the cup of the mouthpiece.

'Hello?'

I put the phone down, appalled at the disappearance of my voice.

This was obviously not very satisfactory. I could not ring again for hours – days, even – or she would guess that I was the hoarse lunatic who had just rung.

Out of my roseate dreams I stepped into the world of waxed floors, squeaky shoes, funfair mirrors and endlessly, endlessly repeated verbal absurdities, where everything I had said or done in her presence was ridiculous, farcical, to be despised and derided. I went to my room and read over my poems. They were hysterical and sentimental, treacly where I had thought them most original; poor, pale, tremulous copies of every romantic poet I had ever read. I tried to read a novel. It might as well have been written in Arabic or Sanskrit. I thought of the traditional consolation of adolescence – the thought repelled me. I was in love. I could not besmirch the image of Helena by that sticky offering.

All day I remained telephonically celibate.

The next day I had begun to recover a little. I went for a walk. To calm my nerves, to summon up courage. I would ring her in the afternoon.

And, a happy omen, the day was considerably warmer. The snow was fast thawing and the trees in the public gardens were laced with rain. A glassed pavilion reflected gold-black clouds. Behind its windows heavy orchids drooped and glistened, their lowered, yawning horns like some mad, soft orchestra of saxophones and trumpets. I thought again of her dark hair, the curious glow beneath her white skin, her brown eyes and red lips.

Gulls beat over the speckled lake.

I had come almost to the centre of this park and was thinking about turning back. I was cured of my temporary madness. I would ring her. I would be positive. It was time to take charge of this affair. To have courage. Once more I was happy. I must have looked odd, smiling to myself as I halted in the middle of the path, turned abruptly, and started to walk in the direction of home.

Tum-tummy-tum-mi-tummy-tum, I hummed. The moisture in the air was turning again to fine rain, but I strode on under the dripping and ticking trees, my head tipped back in joy.

And here, coming along, faces hidden under a huge black umbrella held forward, another pair of happy lovers. A pair of slim white-stockinged legs tripping along to keep up with flapping grey trousers. Approaching, he quickly flipped the edge of the brolly up, presumably to avoid colliding with me. A large, handsome, fleshy mouth flashed me a smile, disappeared again under the black keel. *She* did not see me – I didn't see her face, only her hands interlocked on his arm – but I caught her voice.

'. . . drowned. Oh, Chris, do . . .'

Unmistakable, as they hurried past.

A silvery giggle floated back through the rain.

I continued walking. But my previously springy step had suddenly become jerky and stiff – an incompetently handled marionette. My face, I was sure, was turning from bright red to white to red again as the blood surged and fell away, leaving me alternately engorged, and thin and exhausted. My internal organs had been pulled out and reinserted haphazardly and my skull had been pumped full of molten lead, which had set cold and caused it to loll on its stalk. I stopped. To the air that tasted and smelt of the nearby sea, I added my salt tears. With hair plastered black against my forehead, eyelids inflamed, my new English suit trousers wet through, a pathetically bedraggled, de-winged small bird, I made my dingy way home.

How totally unjust – to be at one moment a virgin, then the next a cuckold, without the compensation of any intervening passion. I stared blindly and ferociously from my window that night. Perhaps her firm, confident grip on his arm did not mean he was her lover. A brother? Cousin? Friend? Perhaps she was deceiving him with me? Even I had to laugh bitterly at that. With his dark skin he was an Italian or something. An obvious seducer. An imbecile without an ounce of poetry in his soul. What the hell had poetry to do with it? Christ – what a whore she was.

But I was still in love with her. A total infatuation – whatever it is called. And the next day I had to return to my school.

It was odd to be returned to an all-male society. But coming back this time was very different. Previously, with all the priggishness of a guilty and resolute masturbator, I had refused to listen to schoolboyish smut. Now I sought out information like a Puritan witch-finder. I discovered to my horror and intense envy that quite a few of my returning contemporaries boasted of 'having it' during the vacation. From the circumstantial details given I was forced to admit to myself that some of their stories might well be true. But, surely, what I had known was love? It had nothing to do with these tales of gropings and fumblings and groaning ecstasy. I withdrew from these sexual narratives. How could I sully my feelings for Helena by talking in that way? I have to admit that I was tempted to invent a mechanical-enough-sounding coupling, but I doubted that my story would stand up. School no longer meant anything to me. But if I was going to be a great poet, I had made a pretty sorry start. I must see my Beatrice, my Leonora again. I stood it for two weeks.

That morning I did not go to class. Borrowing a bicycle from one of the gardening boys I cycled to the nearest village, where there was a telephone in a café.

Strangely, I had no fear in lifting the receiver this time. The local exchange asked me to hold.

The other end seemed to ring for an eternity. Then a woman gruffly answered. The housekeeper?

'Is Helena there?' In three words my voice modulated from panic-high to mature-hoarse.

'A moment, please,' the voice said.

There was a dull thudding and fumbling then, as if the phone had been dropped, picked up and dropped again.

'Hello – Chris?' A girl's voice – not Helena's – blurted on to the line.

'Yes,' I said on impulse.

'Chris – she's not here. We all came back and she wasn't able to get out. Last Saturday she took something and jumped off a chair and everything. Hot bath and everything. God knows, she was ill . . . Hang on . . .' There was a silence for a moment. I imagined a hand held over the mouthpiece. Then the whispering voice rushed on, '. . . and Mama, of course, found out. She went absolutely mad. Packed poor Hel straight off somewhere – she's had a miscarriage.' Silence again.

What was I expected to say? What was a miscarriage?

'Where have you been, though, Chris?' The voice managed to sound both plaintive and forgiving. Before I could say anything however, there came another of those series of bumping and knocking sounds that confirm that the telephone is being transferred, rather messily, from one person to another.

'Helena?' I breathed the name.

'First – ' an altogether older voice – a Mother voice – spoke through the black bakelite ' – let me make it quite clear that Miss van Claes was not, is not and never has been a member of this family. Whatever she has been masquerading as, quite enough time and expense has been taken up by her little adventures. She is no longer with us. Whoever you are, I bid you good-day.'

The line went dead.

When I came out of the café I knew I would not be going back to school. It seemed a simple decision. I picked up the bicycle and pointed it in the opposite direction. A journey of brimming eyes, under high clouds receiving the last of the sun, into an interminable, darkening, flat land. The orange-cratered moon rose, tremendously magnified, at the horizon. When I got into the city, after fifteen kilometres, the moon had been eaten away, and the sky was all over a sulphurous black-yellow, bringing the returning snow. My hair had been steeped up into a ziggurat by the constant, increasingly biting, damp wind.

An apparition to my mother – Father was out somewhere – she had me conveyed immediately to bed. Our maid scampered in front up the stairs – for the first time I noted her hips swinging her navy-blue skirt – myself saying over and over again, 'I'm not going back. Not going back . . .'

In the morning breakfast was delayed. My father had not gone early to the office. He was waiting for me, but clearly chafing under some restriction placed upon him.

'What,' I asked in the middle of their silence, 'is a miscarriage?'

'Now,' said my father, 'perhaps I may speak to my son.'

My mother got up, excused herself, said only, 'Carl?', came over, kissed me on the forehead, and went out of the room.

I stared at my half-eaten breakfast.

My father got up from the table and went across to the sideboard. He selected a cigar from the box and rolled it appraisingly at his ear. He poured a thimble of aquavit and came back to his chair. He cut the end off his cigar – I was going to say circumcised, but that is not accurate – lit it, drew in, and expelled a luxuriant balloon of velvet-blue smoke. He tossed back his little drink, and looked down the table at me. He stood again, and began to speak.

I cannot now remember the exact words he used. He was my father – I discounted most of them because of that.

Somehow he managed to combine the minimum of clinical information with a weighty, but not I think frank, reminiscence of the 'ladies' in his youth. They were divided between the good and the bad. The good he had courted and respected. He had married one such. The bad – had been 'another thing'. The sort every young man must know – and then discard into the bin of time. Did he say that? It sounds like one of my clichés. But, he said, he had always been a gentleman, Cornelius. He leaned back, drew on his cigar, leaned forward again to deposit elegantly the end half-inch of ash on the side of his cleaned plate, and told me to look him straight in the eye. Was there anything I had done – he nodded, as if prompting me – anything at all, that might cause my mother offence, or bring disrepute upon the name of this house? My mother, I must know, would be devastated by any such disgrace, being a good woman.

'No.'

'I knew it.'

He looked fondly at me and came down the table and patted my shoulder forcibly.

'Ah, I knew it. Wish I was your age again, Cornelius. We'd show 'em, eh?' Then he frowned. 'But don't muck on your own doorstep. Understand? Come to your old father if you have any problems.'

He departed cordially for the office.

After dinner that night – my mother retired early – he asked me if I was serious about not going back to school. He seemed in an unusually mellow mood. He had hoped I would matriculate this year, but no matter. It would wait. He had plans. There were more important things than examinations. 'You can join me for a while in the business.'

That was the reason for his good mood. I had made no secret of my despisal of commerce, business – his whole comfortable world. And he had trapped me. With his characteristic good humour and show of interest he had charmed me into agreement, into saying, 'Yes, yes. That would be good for a while.'

A while turned into nearly two years. All that time, behind his consistent good temper, something was gently rocking my father – all of us, like the glasses gently tinkling together in an earth tremor.

He had been planning vaguely for years to open another office in London. Now rumours of war swelled again and he said that we could not wait forever on the whims of the politicians, and went ahead with his plans quickly. He was absent a lot in England from then on. I was his viceroy in the office over here, he said. I was not popular with the staff, but I became adept at the arts of flattery, proud in a way that my father trusted me, while leaving all real decisions to the disposable clerks. That is the way of business.

There is no one better than a cynical, rich young Marxist to run a business. A poet, I kept reminding myself. I am a poet. I drank in the cafés of the capital at night and ordered middle-aged men about in the day over shipments from Indonesia and shipments to Hamburg, and looked on bills of lading with the names of far-off ports with longing. In all the cafés I looked for Helena and armed myself with arguments against what I was doing. And the ports give names to the sea. I know my Auden. And the misprint. The poets give names – only a northern European could let that go. One used to the maps of colonies.

My father spoke to me from London. He was pleased with what I was doing. That made me feel ashamed. And I am ashamed now not to realize how afraid he was, and how he was preparing our exit as gracefully as he could.

Europe, after a brief remission, was hugging its cancers of nationalism. Although she had married a Catholic, my mother's family was solidly Jewish; neither of them made any attempt to follow their religions. And it has haunted me ever since how families like my own could disappear on a day, an instant – a flick of the tails, tap of the wand, the work of a mad illusionist – into ordure and torture – and how the torturers could sustain this horror for day after day, week after week, month after month, and how, only a few weeks, days, hours after the taking of a family like ours from its house, another paterfamilias, not dissimilar to my father, could stand, smoking a cigar, in the window of *their* house, resting his hand benignly on the beautiful sofa he has so fortuitously inherited, while his gentle, charming wife bustles about the kitchen, perspiring a little in the heat from the open oven . . .

In England, my father promised, I was at last to go to University. Before we left, I had one last errand.

One morning, in the late summer of '38, I went out on my bicycle – it had never been returned to the gardener's boy. I found myself in Helena's part of the city. At the archway to her house I stopped and dismounted, wheeling the cycle over the cobbles and under the arch. Across the square, the lower windows of the house were all shuttered as they had been that winter. At the top there were curtains drawn at the middle gable window, but at the end gable the window was bare.

Where did the girl in the high room go to?

The Second Thing

The first time I saw Spencer Benjamin he was sitting on his own at the smallest table in a small, dingy tea-room in Cambridge. He was very pale and tense-looking and for no very clear reason I thought that he might be homosexual. Perhaps it was those extraordinary violet eyes that darkened to a sort of bloody purple later – I understand the film star Elizabeth Taylor has similarly coloured eyes, but I have no way of verifying this. Or his curved bow of a mouth hung between hollowed cheeks. His fine forehead, his long, thick brown hair which was a little too thick and long. When he stood I saw that he was a good six foot tall, his body slim but sturdy as an oarsman's. This was the first – and last – time I observed him drinking tea. A brief while after I made his acquaintance he filled out with alcohol and it improved his appearance.

I didn't speak to him that day. Indeed it seemed that hardly anyone spoke to him. 'The man,' the man who had the room above mine informed me disgustedly, 'is a Fascist. Spouting bloody Roy Campbell's poetry when he came drunk to that party in Donovan's room the other night. He tried to fight everyone there. They threw him out and he sat outside on the stairs bawling and shouting. Man ought to be sent down.'

I agreed – and couldn't have cared less. But then, I was not doing too well socially myself, so perhaps I was ready to be attracted to another outcast. I did not seek Spencer's company, but one evening he came into a little back-street town pub I used, and had thought no one else bothered with. Just an ordinary, working-class place, little used in the evening, where I could sit in a corner and get drunk on tepid bitter and Auden – or whatever other poet I had brought along to read in quiet intoxication. I was tolerated because of my strange accent and the knowledge the English have that all foreigners are insane and best left alone. Anyway, at that time, seven o'clock on a Monday, April evening, I made his acquaintance.

Spencer didn't see me at first. He bustled through the doors, went straight up to the bar, and was served by Edna, the landlady, a slatternly brunette of perhaps thirty-five or eight, with a large bosom and yellow teeth. Spencer began immediately to engage her in a bantering conversation. He leaned confidently on the bar, one foot up on the brass heating pipe. At first his conversation was light, spiced with the sort of semi-sexual innuendo that barmaids must endure every day of their sainted lives; but then I lost touch with what he was saying. His voice had become low and urgent. Edna had come close up on her side of the bar and was listening intently to whatever he was asking, or rather urging. Just then, the curtain at the back of the bar parted, and Edna's small, harassed-looking husband emerged.

It was most well done by the two of them; how Edna transformed herself in one smooth movement into business, energetically wiping the top of the counter, swinging herself away from Spencer, while he banged down his pint glass and drew his hand across his lips, and said with a smile, 'Evening, Jack, I'll have another.'

'Evenin', Spencer. Wife not going on again, is she?'

'No, no,' said Spencer with great bonhomie. 'You've got a good one there, Jack.'

Edna frowned at a spot on the counter and scrubbed harder.

'Umm,' said Jack. 'If you say so.'

I had to admire the practised way Spencer had handled this. For such a young man it was most impressive. A moment ago he had been seducing the landlord's wife; a moment later he was a bosom friend of the landlady's husband.

It was then that Spencer looked round and saw me in the corner. He crossed over. 'I've seen you before . . .' he began.

And so friendships begin. An inequality, perceived by one friend, acknowledged by the other, is one basis. I bought most of the drinks that night, and Spencer swore he would return my hospitality. He never did. He had a room at college on the next but one landing, I learned.

He laughed when I told him about my curious tutor, Mathias.

'All tutors, Cornelius – I may call you that? – are extremely curious,' he said. 'One wonders if they are born or simply grow out of the furniture, the books.'

'They are semi-vegetable,' I agreed.

I told him that I had stopped going to tutorials; that the whole of our academic studies seemed to be an enormous waste of time. The world was going to blow up. I was a poet. What more was needed?

Mathias was my English literature tutor. The first time I went to him, I was at his rooms before him. There was a notice on the door: *Enter – Sit*. I entered and sat on a straight-backed chair before the small, overladen, dusty desk. The room was composed of books and the smell of books and pipe tobacco and a sort of stale biscuity odour that I could not place until I saw the humped form of a black and filthy collie dog, wedged under the window, between a pot plant on a tall bamboo-legged table and a teetering four-square pile of papers and folders at least two feet high. One of the dog's rheumy, red-ringed eyes held me. He growled, but did not move.

I heard Mathias's ankles cracking as he came along the corridor. Each of the weeks I attended, after my statutory hour, I was followed by two boys of about nineteen, who would file in while I was packing away my notes, and sit on the short sofa, its springs grinding flatly under them. They were twins, their faces the colour of white wax candles, with thick wicks of yellow hair. As I went to go, they would rise and bow in unison. Outside in the corridor, I would hear their muffled laughter, and Mathias's high, dry-sherry voice cutting them off.

He was a very small man with a yellow tinge of what looked like cancer on his temples. He would sit facing me in his ancient, lumpy armchair, packed round with black-fringed cushions, a tasselled smoking-cap on his head, forever fiddling with and relighting and letting go out and whistling through and sucking and nibbling at a straight briar pipe as if it was the teat of the ancient milch-cow he called Liter-ature.

It was the nearest, I thought, in the callous way of a young man, that he had ever come to a woman. I once foolishly praised Virginia Woolf in front of him. 'Women have difficulties we can not know about,' he said, blowing a plaintive high note on his pipe. 'Particularly with the art of writing.' He sucked in bubbles.

The only woman he would allow was 'the divine Jane'. 'Jane?' I said stupidly.

'Austen, of course. Austen. Even in your country, surely . . .' He regarded me with loathing.

'Ah, *Mansfield Park*,' I said.

It was an inspired choice. Something remembered as a smile crossed his mouth briefly.

'A brilliant mechanism . . .' He spoke for half an hour on *Mansfield Park*. It is a great book. I wish he had not ruined it for me.

I stopped going to him when he fell asleep as I read an essay. Perhaps, when he awoke, he thought I had been a nasty dream.

I have partly invented him. He was younger, taller, stronger, of some thwarted brilliance. But this was the seed inside him.

I wrote some lines about him:

> The madman in the library breathes
> in humours of peculiar air
> the trepidation of the leaves,
> regards abandoned Europe without care . . .

Etcetera. Etcetera. This, and the rest of it, was printed in a college magazine. When I was out walking, a young man appeared from behind a rhododendron bush and asked if I was the author of the poem. 'That was really rather good,' he said, and disappeared once more into the bush. But it did not make me any more popular, except for this one lunatic.

The pity of these University memoirs is that they are of necessity written by those who can remember, or invent, write and think, and they detail over and over reminiscences of brilliant creatures destined to become poets and novelists and cabinet ministers and rogue financiers and archbishops and police-court cases. What they omit is that sector of the plain, the dull, the bank managers, and remittance men, the metallurgists and solicitors, unregarded by history – anybody's history.

I felt keenly my lack of physical presence and prowess. I still clung to hopes of myself as a famous young poet. Leopardi? Pope? Other great dwarfs? Napoleon? Stalin? Charlie Chaplin? The world was suddenly composed of small, hunched, capering persons. The truth, to the world, was that I was of average height, perhaps a little short, but rather broad and deeply chested. My hair – my proud grey bush now – was then even thicker, impenetrable, black; it stood up and curved forward over my brow like a broom upended. I was fairly strong, but uncertainty and doubt induced a constant physical lassitude which was sparked only by drink. Worst, and most worst of all, I wore the dreadful black, round-rimmed, spider's bicycle of spectacles of the late nineteen-thirties. As worn by Arthur Askey, a well-known comedian and other dwarf of that time.

From my closed window, I watched with envy and contempt more athletic students as they walked silently, sweatered and white shirt-sleeved, gesticulating, under the swagging chestnut trees.

'What is there to do, Spencer?' I wailed. We were each on our fourth outing into the crate of twelve bottled beers.

'It's not quite that bad. The town's not bad. Not bad at all.'

'The Town,' I said sententiously. 'The Town is a collection of public houses each of which surrounds a number of drunken students.'

'I'm not entirely sure your joke is original, Cornelius,' he said. 'Anyway, that's Dublin. It depends what you are looking for. You'll have to come out more. At night. It's time your education was taken in hand, dear Cornelius. Or out of it.'

I accompanied Spencer on many of his hunting trips. In the pubs, tea-rooms, shops, dance-halls, cinemas – everywhere that women were present. It introduced me to Spencer's taste in women; his imperious disregard for such notions as beauty, age and other encumbrances of the poet's temperament; it was the theatre of seduction he loved to conjure – preferably before a companion's eyes.

But, the usual odd couple, we grew close together. As the summer vacation approached, Spencer invited me to come and stay at his family's home in the North.

I was very grateful. Why hadn't it occurred to me to make a reciprocal offer? Then he said, 'Truth is, old boy – it is a little dull up there. You'll liven things up a bit. Besides, there's a girl I don't particularly want to get tangled up with again. I shall plead the necessity of looking after my guest if she becomes too pressing.' As usual Spencer's charity had a solid core of self-interest.

But I was glad to accept. I didn't fancy going to the new house in London and talk of my prospects at the University, chatter of business, my mother's inanities and prying questions about what I was eating, wearing, who my friends were . . .

'Where do you live?' I asked Spencer.

'Northumberland. Strange, woolly place full of strange, woolly people. You'll never have seen anything like. There's nothing to actually do. But we're near the sea. There are some wonderful pubs in the villages up the coast. You can always leave whenever you want. Open house, old dear.'

I asked if he'd mind if I travelled up with him. I really couldn't face going home straight away at the end of term.

So, a few days later, armed with a bottle of whisky for the journey, we slipped out on the morning train to Edinburgh. It was a warm, still day, but apart from us two the carriage was cool and empty. We pulled down the blinds to the corridor, put up the rests so that we could lie full-length on the benches either side of the carriage and devoted the day to whisky, talk, and the cinema the window made of the view.

We passed through the black steel towns and the long moors, Newcastle, which seemed to consist of buildings made of

discarded tombstones and too many bridges. The land flattened
and levelled into a high plain and we sometimes ran along the sea.
Spencer pointed out islands he knew from boyhood. It was
evening. Throughout our journey the sun had swung behind the
train and now, declining, shone across the land, making the
shadow of the train hurry alongside us on the banked track.
'We're almost there,' said Spencer, and began to get his case
down from the rack. I looked forward. The sun, like a gigantic
mellow spotlight, was cast into the curve of the cliffs ahead,
holding the most beautiful view of a village that seemed to tumble
elegantly down from the high cliffs to a low quay and slight,
curved blade of beach. 'Is that it?' I said. 'It looks wonderful.'

'Everything looks wonderful from a train,' said Spencer,
sliding the door open.

Spencer's father was the local doctor. He greeted me warmly. To
my surprise he was a good foot shorter than Spencer, rather fat,
and bald except for a horseshoe shape of grey hair above his ears
and the back of his head. Spencer's mother was tall, with still-
yellow hair brushed severely back from a long, handsome face.
She took an instant dislike to me. And, now entering into the
south-facing drawing-room of that large house halfway down the
hill in the village I had seen from above, was a young woman. An
elderly Labrador dog got off the sofa and ambled to greet her,
raising himself up in an odd, corkscrewing, arthritic movement to
rest his front legs on her chest, his tail lashing and his poor, half-
erect sex wagging.

She was a year younger than her brother, and plainer. Her face
was rather plump, but glowed golden in the evening light that
flooded the front part of the room. Her eyes were large, brown,
frank – quite without her brother's extraordinary colour. Her

lower lip was a small, full, round half-moon betokening sensuality.

(Betokening? Tell me, Mr Pritchard – why do I talk like this? Is it to put some horrible double fence of ironic pomposity between myself and the past?)

'Down, Jake,' she said, pushing in a kindly but firm way her importunate dog down. He looked bewildered for a moment, blinked, then lolloped back and jumped up to his place on the sofa and rearranged himself economically and comfortably and regarded me with a keen interest, his long pink tongue hanging from the side of his mouth.

'Cornelius,' said Spencer. 'My sister, Judith.'

'You must be Spencer's clever friend. Hello.'

We shook hands.

From some effect she had on me, I found myself chattering all the way through dinner. I thought myself brilliant. Spencer laughed. Judith leaned forward, challenging, buoyant, increasingly attractive. Their parents ate solidly on, as if either we, or they, were not entirely there. After the meal they simply vanished into some Northern, middle-aged quietude in another room.

The guest-room was at the top of the house. It was spartan, with a single, old-fashioned hospital bed, with at head and foot two flattened iron hoops like the handles of a giant's tray. The walls were papered with bursts of rather depressed pale-pink roses. There was a dressing-table that appeared to be made out of old floor-boards. A wash-basin with one large tap, marked Cold. It was very much like a room in a cheap, clean temperance hotel.

So my holiday began. And indeed, at first, it did seem like a holiday in a small, slightly disapproving hotel. But after a couple of mornings, at her suggestion, before breakfast, leaving Spencer sleeping late, Judith and I walked down with Jake, through the town and along the narrow beach under the looming sandstone cliff. In the mornings it was cold, with a stiff, implacable breeze blowing off the North Sea. As the dog ran on, Judith dropped behind to talk to me. She was at an art school in Newcastle. She talked about Picasso and the Surrealists. She saw Surrealism in the great loaf-shaped clouds drifting into position overhead. She linked her arm in mine. It was all perfectly innocent – a gesture of friendship. On her part. It surprised me. By the afternoon it would be hot. Spencer came with us to another, gritty beach in a small, lonely bay. The dog sat up amongst the rocks watching us, as he slowly panted. And it seemed to me that Spencer was watching us also, watching me more particularly, with disapproval. Those first long evenings were inevitably slow and wearisome, with Spencer disappearing on mysterious, no doubt erotic errands into the neighbourhood and his parents directing their conversation around me. It was inevitable that I should fall in love with Judith, wasn't it?

In the day she was infuriatingly self-possessed, but let me hold her hand when I sought it under the cover of a towel on the beach as Spencer swam strongly out and back in towards us. When he came back up the beach she would withdraw it – but the second time with a gentle, almost hidden smile. What complicated game was she playing? I planned further steps. She slept beside her parents' room. I would go to her, confess my feelings. She would – what? I was in that puzzled, maddening torment of second, sexual, love, where we replay endlessly every slightest, slighting or encouraging moment like some mad, endlessly rehearsed play in the head.

Spencer and I had already agreed on a night's drinking; it was almost at the end of the week before he was free. We had hardly got a hundred yards up the hill away from the house before Judith came running up behind us, shouting, 'Wait for me. Wait for me.'

'Sally is expecting you to call her,' she said to her brother as we walked along the cliff top. The town lay in a crescent of darkness behind us, the beach grey, the last of the sun lighting the sea far out in deeper and lighter shades of honey-yellow.

'Yes.' He smiled at her. 'Yes?'

They were a little ahead of me on the cliff path, so that I could observe his wolfish smile, her legs striding out in an olive-green, sensible skirt.

'She says you haven't been in touch with her at all,' she persisted accusingly. 'Not even to tell her when you were coming back.'

'She knows the vacation dates.'

'You should have written.'

At last we came to the next bay.

A few large houses perched halfway down the cliff. A grey church like a sleeping owl squatted lower down, its clock showing the wrong time. Then a street of brown brick, then of white-faced cottages. Pebbles fell away down the steep incline from under our feet. By the time we reached the small quayside pub I felt that she was my girl – the only one who would certainly never be Spencer's.

The pub was purely a local one for fishermen and farmers and such-like; but even here Spencer was known and greeted, in a low, slightly grudging, but not unfriendly way at the bar. At first I felt like a parcel they had brought with them. We sat at a small round oak table, forced into propinquity. And as we drank pint after pint of heavy, dark bitter, Spencer and Judith and I seemed to become one endlessly understanding single organism and the frowsty small bar twisted and vanished away in the blue-brown cloud of smoke that hovered over us, and only our jokes, our conversation, our understanding, ourselves existed in the whole world.

When we came out the village was a stage-set after a show. The flat-walled, banked street lifting up to the starry sky was rapidly deserted as we went up, the few late drinkers hurrying away up alleys that quickly dissolved them into darkness. No lights on, lives that hardly existed behind the moon-paled exteriors, sleeping at best. How could I know? – why should I know? – the sheer vigour, decay, life of others – the men in vests and underpants clambering aboard their beds, their wives and girls waking, complaining, drifting again to sleep, the snores, late cups of thick tea stirred, the curtains twitched to, the little windows opened to the night air, closed against the night air. To a philosopher nothing is quite real. Say that again. To a philosopher nothing is real that is not demonstrated. Again. None of those whole, hale, easy-muscled, cramp-tortured, demon-ridden, cancer-nascent, loving, unloving, hated, loved bodies are real. Were real.

The village melted into night behind us. We gained the cliff again. The moon gleamed like a medal high over the sea. The sea was a quiet army of assassins, teeming with silver knives.

We floated on the cliff. The walk was three miles back. The first gross feeling of beeriness wore off – but not my new-found euphoria. Spencer hung back, but then, with a grunt, swung himself ahead of us, so that we saw his square body mounting resolutely and somehow sullenly before us on the slow incline. Judith and I had our hands locked. She giggled as he went up and down and out of sight.

My arm went round her waist – surprising how much heavier and stronger even slight-seeming women turn out to be when you take hold of them – and we shared, ardently, a long kiss. The huge sky rounded above. The night air lay heavy and warm. The stars were brilliant and singular as I had never seen them before. We drew apart at last, and a shout came from Spencer, 'Come on.' With her head resting against my shoulder we walked on, an amiably amorous four-legged beast.

Now we came to their town. Coming towards the house, she detached herself from me and looked up into my face. She smiled. We kissed again in the middle of the street. 'I didn't know you were like that,' she whispered.

'Eh? Like what?' I was puzzled.

'Sorry.' She laughed. 'From what Spencer said . . .'

She did not go on. It took me a little while to sort out the imputation of homosexuality in her words. Did Spencer really believe that? That that was the reason I clung to him? Had he wanted to add another, perverse admirer to his person? Or did he simply find it amusing to tell his sister about his queer friend? How many others, dear God, had he told? But all of this later, much later, after she had again taken me by the hand and led me into the house.

We burst buoyantly into the kitchen. Spencer was talking with his mother at the table. They both fell silent and looked at us. The mother, with a strange, reproachful stare at Judith, said, 'I suppose you and Spencer's guest would like some supper?'

'Good time?' Spencer asked sarcastically, as he led me through the hall into the drawing-room.

We sat down and did not talk. Judith came in a few minutes later carrying a tray with three cups of milky cocoa. The mother put her head round the door. 'I shall say goodnight,' she said, managing to avoid looking at me. 'I'm sure you would all like to get to bed – and your father won't want to find you up if he comes home tired from his call.'

So we sat, Spencer and I in those deep, enveloping armchairs, Judith perched on an arm of mine, silent, the long windows open to the garden because of the warmth of the night. Spencer set down his cup first.

'I'd better show you to your room, Cornelius.'

One cannot really complain and demand, half drunkenly, to be allowed to stay up late in someone else's house.

Judith smiled down at me.

'Thanks,' I said a little too loudly to Spencer.

'What a funny way to end an evening,' Judith said in the direction of her brother.

'It's been a wonderful evening,' I protested. 'You are so fortunate to be here. To live here.'

'We're only on holiday, like you,' said Spencer. He stood at the door waiting for me.

'Goodnight, Judith.'

'Goodnight, Cornelius.'

'In the morning, old chap.' A large, not entirely unfriendly warder, Spencer stood in the doorway of the bedroom.

'In the morning,' I replied. And he departed, closing the door with a loud click.

Unable to bear the room, I turned off the light and pulled back the curtain on the small dormer window.

I sat on the edge of the bed. I felt, as if she still held it, the touch of Judith's hand in mine. The feel of her lips, tongue, small, sharp teeth. The very weight and contours of her body. The scent that rose from between her breasts, the scent mixed with the still, salt air . . . Again, the fold and roll and press of her body, the form and firmness of the leg pressed between mine as we kissed.

I lay on my back watching the white ceiling. And her recent memory lay, a light incubus, covering me.

At last I sat abruptly up and pulled off my shoes and socks. I draped my trousers over the dressing-table. The alcohol had become a pleasant warmth, the blood-sugar pumped, making my nerves intensely alive; I slid under the sheet.

The room was lit palely by the brilliant moon. I watched the black corner of the dressing-table. It was the prow of a black boat setting sail into night. The room dimmed, brightened, dimmed again. My eyes closed. My mind full of images of love, I began to drift towards sleep.

The door was opening. The door was closing. In a short white gown, her naked legs white – she seemed at first far away and then at my side – she slid under my welcoming arch of arm and sheet and into the narrow bed. Fuseli. All my responses are aesthetic now.

Then? 'Judith,' I breathed.

I came down the next morning a little late; too late for breakfast. I walked through the empty dining-room, the table cleared, and out into the garden. I caught a glimpse of myself in the open kitchen window. My skin had tanned in the salt wind; my hair, normally slicked down, floated in a dark, waving bush – the floating hair, the flashing, bespectacled eye! From the kitchen I heard voices raised indistinctly in argument. Judith and her mother. I crept almost up to the window, my feet crunching on the gravel path. I heard Judith shout, 'What has he to do with it? I will see who I please.' The bang of a door inside. I came past the window. Her mother's face, with a red spot of anger under each high cheek-bone, stared out at me, then turned abruptly away.

As I came to the corner of the house, Judith dashed out of the front door. I called to her. She shook her head violently and half-ran down the path and out of the gate. She stalked on, down the street towards the sea.

I did not go after her as I should have done. It was obvious she wished to be alone. But I, considering myself as her lover – I should have pursued her. A gull shrieked overhead, reproving my timidity. Being in Paradise, you see, at least on a visit, I thought I could understand all the creatures there.

The road to the sea was closed by Judith's anger. Spencer was out. The house, the back at least, was in the hands of their mother. I had no money or cigarettes. I had to go back in to get anything. I went in boldly by the front door and slipped upstairs to my room. I opened the window fully and lay down on the mattress.

The day was still. I lay in a strange house, in a strange town, and wondered about Judith's behaviour. It sounded as if she had been arguing about me. That was flattering, if a little alarming. The rather fumbling and not entirely satisfactory encounter last night must have meant more to her than to me. That is, we are taught, always the way with women. On the basis of my lately lost virginity I considered myself an expert. I sighed. Ah, complications, complications. The cool breeze lifted and let drop the curtain. The gulls shouted raucously, rising and falling like boozy angels outside the window. It was a pity I could not seek Spencer's advice – but she was his sister, and he had hardly seemed approving in any measure last night. Ah, if he had known. I made up my mind. I would go and find Judith and say – what? Far down in the house the telephone began to ring, as it often did in this doctor's house.

The ringing stopped. I thought no more of it.

There was a sound of someone mounting the stairs. A gentle knocking on the door. Judith.

I jumped from the bed. Judith's mother stood on the landing. For the first time she looked fully into my face. 'Cornelius. Can you come down? There is a telephone call for you. Please don't worry.'

There is, I have read, an instant before one hears bad news when one has a pre-vision, a pre-echo rather, of what one is going to hear. When time loops charitably back on itself to warn, to prepare.

I followed her downstairs. She handed me the telephone.

First, my mother's voice, sounding oddly strained, said, 'Cornelius. Is that you, Cornelius? Dadda – ' then she dissolved into sobs. (There must be somewhere some retribution for writers who so calmly discuss these things. Somewhere in the Inferno, we are kept chattering brightly amongst ourselves.) The phone was taken from her. (One of the things we talk about is the telephone as a conduit for sudden plot changes.)

Another voice. A man's – with that horrible mock-refined accent so many English southerners have, where they throw the words to the back of the throat, half-strangle them there, then obstruct their egress by raising and keeping the tongue to the middle of the palate.

'Mr Marten? Are you there?' The miserable voice hunted for me down the wire.

'Yes, yes. Where is my mother? What has happened?'

'It's your father actually, Mr Marten. Mr Marten? We had an awful job finding where you were.'

'What?'

'I'm afraid your father has been taken very ill.'

'How?' He had been ridiculously well the last time I had seen him.

'A heart attack,' the voice resumed. 'At the office. Just after we opened yesterday.' A pause. 'I'm terribly sorry to have to be the one to tell you this. Your father has, I'm really most terribly sorry, but your father has passed away.'

I was looking straight into the face of Judith's mother.

She helped me to start packing, when I had put down the phone with a sort of sleepwalker's deliberateness. Into my room first Judith, then Spencer, and lastly their father infiltrated themselves and stood around like characters on a stage. They were suddenly unreal and peripheral and, like all in such roles, knew it. I was the true, the suffering Hero, clad in tragedy.

There was an evening express from Newcastle. Accompanied by Spencer and Judith, the father drove me down in his car. Once on the train, I felt nothing. I stared out of the window. They stood on the platform. The train jerked forward. Judith waved half-heartedly, Spencer raised his hand in manly salute. The father consulted his watch. They began to walk forward slowly in time. As the train pulled out, their hands fell and they turned away.

It was midnight when I reached the house in London. Mother was by now composed. She said that my father had gone to the office yesterday at the usual time early in the morning. She had seen him next that afternoon in the mortuary at Charing Cross hospital. I kissed her goodnight. She would stay up. Without my father in the house I felt as if I had come to another stranger's house. An odd night: snatches of sleep alternated with floating dreams of my father as he had been when I was a child. Images of Judith's face close and pale in the dark. His head of greying hair, with his back to me as he talked in some language I could not understand.

His body was brought back to the house the next day – at my mother's special request. She would not have him lying in some mortician's parlour. He was in the drawing-room. I went in to him.

The coffin was open. His face looked drawn and very much older and curiously blue, as if he had fallen and somehow bruised both of his cheeks. I kissed his forehead. It was impossibly cold.

Another night I lay above his upturned face.

I came down and found the coffin lid closed and fixed down. A circle of red and white carnations lay on top. Undertakers, as black and self-abasing as moles, hid behind doors and curtains; their black gloves, like conjurers', produced white, black-edged cards, white flowers, more flowers, more cards, placing them in an elaborate game on the coffin and the table on which it lay.

Friends of the family, employees of the business began to arrive. They paid court to my mother. They shook my hand. Sometimes both of my hands. They conversed in low voices. I looked out of the window. It was a fine day. I watched a chaffinch bob down a long spike of hawthorn hedge, using the thorns as the rungs of a ladder.

Then it was time for the funeral.

The ground was dry and sandy and dribbled between the upright planks when the coffin was lowered. I found myself thinking of Judith and that I would not see her again. That I did not particularly want to see her again. They say no one is a man until his father dies. I had been informed that morning of the small fortune to come from my father's estate.

And back at the house the senior members of the staff at Father's office gathered round me. Their hair was brilliantined, their black shoes shone. They stared round gratefully, to see if their pensions were hung in the pictures on the walls, whether the antique furniture was fake or real. Two men in particular clung to each side of me.

'We just wanted you to know, Mister Cornelius, that if there is anything we can do to help . . . must express our heartfelt commiserations,' said the one with a ginger moustache.

'Heartfelt,' echoed his accomplice – a flat, bald skull, with pieces of black hair on each side like parentheses. 'Your father was a fine man.'

'Indeed he was,' said the ginger moustache.

'You must,' I said, 'be hot in those suits, gentlemen. Let me help you to a drink.'

They followed, sweating and grateful, to the gin-laden sideboard.

In that long room, full of the sad, the jovial and the paid-for, my mother sat regally in black in a tall, straight-backed chair. I knew for the first time the power that a little money can wield. The two men padded at my heels, whispering their hopes for the business, listening with urgent attention to my ignorant suggestions; when I made a small joke about the uncertainty of the ground at my father's graveside compared to both the international situation and the state of business generally, they at first looked at each other, then dutifully and dreadfully smiled in a sickly way. I thought how it was in my gift to throw these men away – until I heard what my mother had to say at our melancholy cold supper alone that night.

She reproved me when I fetched the brandy decanter from the sideboard. I protested – forgive me, Mama, but Father often used to help me to a drink himself. She replied, with a wholly new sharpness, that it did not matter what he had done – but if I could not pass a day without drinking like a pig – she had observed me since I came home – then I had better seek companions and quarters elsewhere.

I sat dumbfounded at the table. I must admit that I was not close to her. She had paraded me as a child – I remember her horror when my father caught me squinting at the clock in the drawing-room after he had asked me the time. They took me the next day to an oculist, who immediately discovered that I was short-sighted.

'His eyes will be all right?' asked my mother, greatly agitated. 'There is no danger?'

'No, no,' he reassured her. 'Spectacles will correct his vision.'

That was when her real look of horror came. 'Spectacles? He will not have to wear them all the time, surely?'

'Except when he sleeps or is asleep. Or to see or read,' he said sardonically.

'But,' she persisted, pleading, 'not always, surely?'

The thought of her son being enclosed in those steel monsters . . .

But well now, this was ridiculous. I could do nothing but sit there without a drink.

She told me that the business was entirely in her control now. That I had neither the experience nor the right to interfere with it. That I should concentrate on my studies at the University. How else was I to prove myself?

I did not tell her then of my decision not to return to college. I put her sudden sharpness down to grief. But I realized that I had never really known either of my parents – least of all the one who was left. In the days that followed she grew a little mellower. When she stopped talking, she would be looking into the distance as if it were the past. I was too young to understand grief – I have always distanced myself from such things. But as she grew quieter, she grew more possessive. It was as if, my being the only man left in the house, she craved my company, but at the same time took a perverse pleasure in comparing all my actions, mannerisms, looks and ambitions unfavourably to my father's.

'When he was twenty-one he already had a business of his own. We were engaged at twenty-two. Oh – you're going out again?' And I would leave her poring over the ledgers my father had so immaculately kept; looking for his life in the black script between the thin blue and red lines.

Please tell me if I am repeating myself. We must get on. Where?

Ah, Judith. She is not disposed of yet, is she?

I should have rung her on the night I got back – to gain the kudos that suffering brings to the romantic lover in literature. After the funeral. When I had settled down at home. But the day passed. A week. Almost two. Poor Judith seemed very far away. Why did I think 'poor Judith'? Perhaps there was a certain pleasure in feeling a little cruel. One day a car came to take Mother down to the office. I was alone. I rang. I had had a few drinks.

Spencer answered. 'Hello. Hello. Who?' Did he really not know me, or was he pretending in that slightly malicious, jokey way? 'Oh, Cornelius – how good to hear from you. Sorry about your . . . No, she's not here. Well, here, of course, but not here at this moment. I will. When she comes in. Why? No, I won't say you love her – '

'Well, she knows. You know . . .' I said thickly, triumphantly.

'Cornelius – it's time somebody told you. Eh? Told you. Judith has a fiancé. A fiancé. She's engaged to be married. She has been for a year. No, I don't know why she didn't tell you. I was going to, but . . .'

Perhaps, at the age of twenty-one, it was time to stop being a fool.

The Third Thing

In the war I made up stories. I had not wanted to talk about the war. In all the foregoing I have left out our earnest discussions about Fascism, the inevitability of History. But then this whole narrative is about avoidance – of emotional, of political commitment, of that inevitable History that suddenly threatened to overtake us so horribly and unfairly. It is about all the things that happened on the level where we really live – where I lived, for that is all I can know, and in that it is true, and in that it is a lie; for we cannot resist justifying ourselves against all the evidence. Not to try to do so would be too painful. For our ears only then, as Wolfson, the boss of the Fictional Lives Section, used to say, bending forward confidentially over his desk. And for yours and mine only, Mr Pritchard.

Let us get on then, with this list of things that any biography will leave out, because only I know how they happened to me, and any witnesses will tell you their lives and I shall only be a character in them. For instance, Spencer is dead, so that any of my conversations with him must be taken on trust. Judith will never tell that she shared my bed – even if she remembers. Helena is gone forever. Dorothy can tell you about my meals, drinking and sexual habits – but only she is, or was this morning, around. The rest of a life is this nonsense of dates and glimpses by the outside world. I cannot think of a single biography that suggests that the subject in any sense lived. They are a series of records; not a recording. On with the recording.

The late summer of 1939 was radiant. Everyone was anxious about the threat of war. No one would say it was coming – it seemed that if only we kept quiet it would go away. It was as if a man was knocking, knocking at the door, but if we all held our breath for long enough he would at last be convinced the house was empty.

Thus we came to the war's eve. Its first day. And nothing happened. Oh, to the Poles – but not to us. Obscure Finns obscurely battled obscurer Russians for a snow-obscured frontier woolly-red with blood. The English admired the Finns as underdogs. My friends deplored their politics. But there was no danger for us. After a while it seemed that the whole dream might go away.

A few months later some of those friends had already disappeared into the Army – to reappear weeks later in identity-confusing uniforms. Their hair was cropped shorter, eyes brighter; they had an air, at first, of sheepish self-consciousness, but then a steadily growing air of patronizing contempt for us defensively cynical outsiders.

For that winter and the succeeding spring I pursued girls and bottles at girl and bottle parties. I nursed still a congestion in my breast, a warm, milky feeling in my brain, that told me I was a poet. Some of my undergraduate efforts appeared in little magazines. I haunted the pubs of Fitzrovia in search of dragons and centaurs, in the reign of Dylan the First. I always grew confused in the '60s when people referred to 'Dylan', meaning the Second. Once, in America, I was introduced, against my will, to a record of the second Dylan. 'This,' said my torturer, 'is the poetry of Now.' Then.

In the short afternoons of that winter and the following spring I would sit for hours in my high bedroom, smoking and staring out over the bits of Hampstead I could see. In between cigarettes I amassed enough poems for a slim volume. War is a good time for poets – their books consume little paper and effort to produce. But, oh, no cynicism *then*. Though half of the edition was stacked on my bedroom floor, it was as if a scent of the future – a future quite different from the one being prepared outside – rose from its thick, uncut pages, its pink-grey cloth.

I waited for fame. Friends were kind. Some of them, those for whom I had bought drinks, reviewed it kindly. Its title, *The Perjured Chameleon*, rapidly settled itself as a joke. 'What was it, Cornelius? *The Perverted Comedian*?' A few weeks later it was forgotten. Instead of fame, an invitation to the war arrived in a brown envelope.

I was ordered to report to a church hall in Camden Town. There was a queue of men, cloth-capped and soft-hatted. Only the very young were bare-headed. A thin haze of fresh, blue cigarette smoke hung across the general atmosphere of grey, stale cigarette smoke.

A harassed-looking corporal in, I noticed despondently, wire-rimmed spectacles – I wouldn't get out of it that way – hurried amongst us, saying, in a refined, rather effeminate voice, 'Line up. Line up, please. You are all M's, aren't you? All M's?'

'No – B's, mate. Silly B's,' said the man in front of me, drawing a general laugh, and turning to expose a set of chronically rotten teeth. He was obviously putting down an early marker for the role of barrack-room comedian. A good sort. Bit of a laugh. Necessary for discipline, sar'nt-major. Release the tension. A character. I shrank at the thought of spending what was left of my life in the same billet as him.

At last organized, called forward in rows of four, we stripped. A doctor strode purposefully from a side door. His tense, cold fingers tapped on our chests, clasped our throats, touched like fiery ice behind our ears. He went round the back of our rank and we had to present first one, then the other foot for his farrier's inspection.

'Eyes all right apart from the glasses?'

Nod.

'Oh dear. Had trouble with these?'

My feet.

The trouble was, they were flat. I had never felt anything was wrong with them, but when the doctor released me I hobbled over to my clothes as if I had boards strapped to my feet. I waddled home.

'What are you going to do then?' asked my mother tartly.

I drank. I went out. I started a novel about a young man living in London. I wrote reviews of books I would never read. Went with girls.

Ah, the girls. A sampling. Yvonne – flute player, member of a Trotskyist group against whom all the world, including me, conspired. A fat Austrian girl whose name escapes me – Hilda? – who insisted that I looked poetic and thin and that I must be fed, sitting opposite me in the Corner House, her eyes devouring me as I picked my way fastidiously through Shepherd's Pie. And Primavera. She was beautiful in a reptilian way, with large, wide eyes whose lids blinked quickly and alarmingly. She regarded me as 'insufficiently mentally pure', and was most shocked and reproving when I attempted to do no more than kiss her closed, or rather, clenched mouth. I could see why Spencer had preferred waitresses and barmaids.

I thought of Spencer sometimes. Not Judith. I imagined him, face blackened with burnt cork, clambering at dead of night up foreign jetties, inches only from the unknowing sentry's jackboots. Or bucketing across desert dunes in an open Jeep, his hair flung back by the wind. Then, turning up again in London, superbly dashing in a Captain's uniform. Why a Captain I cannot say, except that it seemed the most romantic of ranks – neither the callowness of a subaltern, nor the pomposities of command.

The point was that everyone else seemed to be starting something. I reviewed my life to date. I was twenty-two years old. I had disappointed my mother by not being my father. I had money. I had a toehold in the reduced London literary world. I had written one book and started several others. But I had no job. When the whole world was busy I had no occupation. It was yet another insult to be constantly reminded by my mother of how

Father would have acted. I began to wonder if I would ever be capable of performing any useful act whatever.

Then I had a letter.

A porter dressed in a bottle-green uniform with a row of medal ribbons lurched towards me in the Ministry's echoing tiled vestibule that looked like an enormous lavatory. I somehow assumed he would smell of drink – being at the age when we ascribe comic features to the old – and was ashamed to see that one of his legs was shorter than the other. He studied my letter. 'Yuss,' he said at last, 'that would be room 210. Show you the way, sir. Way, sir.' He began to go up the great iron-railed staircase. He seemed quite agile and I wondered if his deformity had not been caused by years of going up and down the stairs in this way, so that he kept himself half turned to me in a curious deferential manner as he hauled himself up the banister with one hand, beckoning me upwards with the other. I wondered at the sight his trousers must make hung in a wardrobe. And where did one buy lop-sided clothes? And did he even have a wardrobe? By the top of the stairs I had placed him in a small bedsitter of cared-for squalor. We are also insufferably patronizing when young. He continued to refer to the letter as he crabbed on to the landing and along a corridor, as if to constantly remind himself of his destination.

A series of heavy oak doors with brass numerals. 200, 202, 204 . . . 210. He advanced to the next, 212. 'This is where you want for there, sir,' he said, pointing back to 210. He opened the door and, standing back to let me enter, announced, 'A gentleman, Mr Morton.'

The very beautiful girl sitting at the desk was in WRACS uniform. She put a fingertip delicately on the name written in an otherwise empty page of the large desk diary at the side of her typewriter. 'Morton? Oh, you must be Mr Marten.'

I can remember exactly how subtly she stressed the words in that short sentence:

> *You* must be Mr Marten
> You *must* be Mr Marten
> You must *be* Mr Marten
> You must be *Mr* Marten
> You must be Mr *Marten*

so as to leave me with the impression that she had stressed them all, implying simultaneously my extreme unimportance, her professional subservience; my luck at arriving at her door, her complete indifference; surprise that I was like what I was; knowledge that she knew very clearly who I was; our relative worth; and her own effortless superiority, occasioned by her beauty, which though fleeting and temporal, was far in excess of any natural gifts I might have . . .

I gave her the letter. She put it down without reading it. 'If you would just wait for one moment, Mr Marten.'

She got up and crossed the room and knocked on a connecting door to 210. There was a minimal wait.

She opened the door and let a languid, 'Come . . .' float through.

'Sorry . . .' she murmured.

'Um?'

'. . . o'clock . . . Marten . . . see you.'

'Ah.'

She stood aside, flattening herself – as much as her deliciously curved body would allow – against the door, turning a ravishing smile to me, as the man in the office pushed back his chair with a loud scrape and swept out past her.

Spencer.

'Cornelius. How grand.' He seized my hand and stared into my eyes. 'Looking a bit peaky, old chap. But come in. Come in. Gwenda, there's a love, get a couple of drinks for us, will you?'

Gwenda came in after us and shut the door.

'Gin OK?' he asked. She busied herself among the bottles and glasses arrayed on top of a low bookcase. 'Bit early in the day for Scotch, and the smell is not quite so, so . . . ?'

'Redolent,' I said mechanically, sitting down in the armchair in front of his desk. The leather sank like a lift, and I found myself, ridiculously, with my chin almost on a level with the surface of his desk.

'Of what though, Cornelius? Of what? Adjective surely? Redolent of what?'

'I thought you were searching for a word.'

He frowned in a puzzled way, his thick bars of eyebrows almost meeting. Then he smiled. He had decided not to be annoyed, it seemed. Like many who imagine themselves friends, we in fact inhabited mutually exclusive worlds. He peered into mine.

'Well, then – how are you keeping? We haven't seen each other for, what, a year? Almost a year.' He lit a cigarette from a box on the desk. 'Sorry.' He pushed the box across.

We sat in a matey cloud of mating cigarette smoke. Gwenda gave me a tall glass of gin and lime; as she leaned over me the drink's sharp scent mingled with a faint, warm whiff of her perfume. She slid away and left us alone.

'Over a year. Must be.'

'Yes. To tell you the truth, I thought you'd be in the Army or something, Spencer. Leading raids on the enemy, all that sort of thing.'

Ah, did I not tell you that France had fallen, around the time of the publication of my poems? What was that joke about the pompous novelist, Charles Morgan? *I spent thirty years perfecting the use of the colon – then the war came.*

'Commandos, you mean,' he said. 'Well – perhaps later. At the moment what we're doing here is rather hush-hush. I can tell you more if you agree to join us.'

'If it's Army, I have to tell you that they've refused me once.'

'No, it's not Army. What for? Eyes?'

'Feet.'

He laughed. 'Not Army as such. We don't wear uniform – Gwenda does, and some of the runabouts – but you wouldn't. You wouldn't have the rank, anyway. You'd be still a civilian. Have some more gin.'

That is a drinker talking. 'More' instead of 'another'.

We had several more gins. The morning unwound. He gossiped, telling me about the job – propaganda, background information, pamphlets, film-scripts. 'Lunch,' he announced.

'I know a chap with a whole cellar full of good stuff still,' he said. Spencer always knew a chap with something or other to offer him. The chap had a small French restaurant. The food was not very good.

'The whole brief of the department is why our side is better than their side. God with us, not *Gott mit uns*. Not that exactly either. Old hat now. We have discovered the common man, Cornelius. The common man is going to have to fight this war. What's more, the idea of him is going to have to fight this war. Our idea of him.'

I yawned as the claret mixed with the office gin.

'That's the open side of it, at least. There is more secret work. I think you can help us.' One of his huge hands reached over the table and clamped my shoulder, shaking it in rough affection. 'What we need is a fluent – native – speaker of your language.

And writer – quite important that. Someone with imagination. I
have been asked – ' his voice dropped ' – if I knew of anyone just
come over here. Anyone good. And of course, I thought of you.
When I mentioned your name the Colonel said he'd heard of you.
Now how could he have done that?'

'My poetry . . .' I suggested facetiously.

'Maybe. Maybe. He is a publisher in civvy street,' he said
thoughtfully. 'By the way, I enjoyed *The Black Camellia*,
Cornelius. Very much.'

'*Perjured*,' I said. '*Chameleon*.'

'Eh?'

'It doesn't matter.'

'You'll come in with us?'

'Delighted.'

You note that I had said nothing about Judith; he had
volunteered no information. I had also done him a small favour, I
thought. I was learning the codes of behaviour.

So I entered my first employment by others. And by so doing, I
discovered something rather alarming about myself – that I
enjoyed being made use of, and being a party to all the little
intrigues of office politics. I even, for God's sake, liked the
frowsty office with its crosses of sticking-plaster across the
window, its fly-papers and brown teapot and boredom. The work
to which I was put – the translating of propaganda leaflets into my
native language – obviously excluded Spencer from inspecting its
competence or accuracy. I had a desk in 210 – it meant that he
was frequently absent. On only my third day there I found myself
breathing assurances down the telephone to some woman that,
no, Mr Benjamin would not be back until very much later, if at
all, but, yes, if I did see him, yes, I would get him to call back. As
soon as he came in. And, as I spoke, Spencer leaned against the

jamb of the office door. I replaced the receiver and a look of relaxed, amused complacency filled his face.

'Well done, Cornelius. I can see you're going to be a godsend.'

So we went to war.

In the autumn of the following year the war came overhead with a vengeance every night, went away in the day; a massive, overturning, restless nightmare. In the lull that came after the alarm siren and just before a big raid I went with Spencer up to the roof of the Ministry. The city was blacked out but a horribly full moon covered the roofs and shone on the upper windows. London lay, spectrally beautiful under the moon, humped, seemingly asleep, like a woman pretending as her lover watches her, while the light of the fire flickers across her body. 'It must be,' I said rather crassly, 'the first time since Shakespeare's time that the city has lain so completely in darkness.'

He was silent; he stared exultantly upwards. 'It is a great time,' he breathed. The sirens began to wail again and the searchlight beams shot up into the sky and began to search. There came the first steady crump-crump of bombs from the east, down by the river. He took his foot from off the parapet and smiled at me. 'A great time, Cornelius.' He laid an arm tenderly across my shoulders. 'Come on, we'd better see you tucked up for the night . . .'

The war was the time for such friendship – and for love. One thing I had not mentioned. I had met Dorothy. She worked as a typist in Room 215, the Pool.

At first I was tentative in my approaches. My experience, half-drunk and fumbling, the night with Judith, had left me a technical non-virgin, but I was still mortally afraid of rejection. I took to dropping into the office early and going into 215 for the first pot of tea. As likely as not, Dorothy would be the first there. She told me she had to leave early because of the long bus journey from her parents' house somewhere out in the suburbs.

She was a little older than me, rather thin, with a bright, sharp face, a tiny nose and a straight, unsensual mouth. You will recognize her to this day from that description. But she had a hard, bright sense of humour, a sometimes cruel, but good mind, and surprisingly large breasts. When I was not co-opted into Spencer's long, liquid lunches, I would take her to a small, plain café. We visited bookshops, the cinema, galleries. It was a while before she would agree to come out at night; then it was pubs, pubs, and sometimes a concert or theatre. Oddly, of the affairs I detail here, I remember less of that one in its early days. It was in all ways a cooler undertaking.

My solitary drinking, the fear and boredom that occasioned that, lessened now that I had a companion. We became lovers only after several weeks – in a hotel room I had booked for the afternoon. She was, again, a rather cool and deliberate lover and I acquitted myself adequately, gaining in confidence. We revisited the same room several times. But when I suggested it for the sixth or seventh time, she said no, she didn't want to go back there.

'I thought you'd grown fond of the old place,' I said.

'Not that fond,' she said. 'I don't want to be taken for granted. I think if you want me, you had better find somewhere for us, don't you?' Shocked, I thought I had lost her, and realized I didn't want to lose her. 'I will – of course,' I said. 'That will be much better,' she said. I set out to find a flat.

And I had waited nervously for Dorothy to mention Spencer. Though she could not be called Spencer's 'type' – whatever that was – I knew that he had fished energetically among the girls in the Pool. His was the cheerfully catholic sexual appetite that does not consider peripherals of age or appearance – 'I would, Cornelius,' he said to me one day, 'fuck a goat if it presented itself to me in the proper way.' In bed, on our second meeting in the hotel room, I discreetly canvassed Dorothy's opinion of my friend.

'Oh, Spencer? I really can't stand those hearty back-slapping chaps.'

'A hearty?'

'Exactly. A kulak.'

'Kulak?'

'A petty bourgeois adventurer.'

Ah. I supposed he was. Dorothy was, of course, a communist. We all were.

However, and whatever she thought of him, he soon came across us together in the pubs. The three of us, four of us with his current girl-friend, spent quite a lot of time together. Whenever they met, Dorothy was admirably cool towards him, and seemed to grow cooler as the weeks passed and Spencer took to dropping round to the flat I had taken for her in Holloway – I was still living with Mother and only spent some nights at the flat. Once, arriving about seven one evening, I found Spencer waiting for me. The atmosphere seemed rather strained. After he had had a couple of drinks and gone, I chided Dorothy humorously. 'You might at least have been polite to poor Spencer.'

'Poor Spencer!'

'You hardly spoke to him at all. The poor fellow hardly knew what to say. You did embarrass him a little, you know.'

'Tch.' She clicked her tongue in disgust. Then gave an odd, high laugh. 'That is the least of his problems, I should think,' she said.

For the first time in my life I was truly happy. The flat was in a modern block built just before the war, one of several above a row of rather chi-chi shops – Madame Yolande Fashions was below us, I remember. We were two floors up – across the road were the blue-tiled roofs of solid Edwardian villas. We were also far enough out to miss the bombing. And close enough to my mother's so that I could slip away late at night. Mother glared at me in the mornings. I was pushed into further action by Spencer.

He had kept out of the office for a couple of days. Then he came breezing in and sat down at his desk. He flicked through some papers – he never had many. I buried myself in a pamphlet on the post-war reconstruction of the dairy industry in the Low Countries.

'This thing with Dorothy,' he said suddenly. 'Lasting, is it?'

'Yes – I think it is.'

'This flat – are you living with her?'

'Yes,' I said, not quite accurately.

'Um – thing is, old boy. Not quite kosher that. Civil Service frowns rather on living in sin between members of the staff. I don't mind in the slightest. But it'll come out sooner or later from some bloody busybody or other. What are you going to do?'

'I don't know.' I laughed. Prudery – from Spencer?

'I'm serious,' he said sternly. 'No can do.'

'Oh.'

He lit a cigarette without offering the packet as he usually did when we were alone.

'Why don't you marry her? Much the simplest thing.'

'I suppose it is.'

'Besides, you never know with this bloody war, do you?'

So it was that spring evening I asked Dorothy to marry me.

'Yes, all right. Why don't we?' she said, or something equally banal.

We sat on the window-seat for a long time, talking quietly as the night fell outside. Though that is not true. It does not fall: it grows up from the ground. While the sky is lit still at its height, shadows creep up the faces of the houses and drown them and only at last the high, cold cocks on the churches burn fiercely, then they are extinguished too.

We went to bed.

It is day that falls. The world lifts out. It begins in the roof of the air, catching the swallows' bellies, the same spires, comes down the same walls, exposing; from the window of the flat's bedroom I watched the street grow radiant once more.

With our engagement announced – though Dorothy would not submit to a ring – I felt able to move in with her. We had not set a date for any ceremony. More importantly, I had not yet told Mother.

I did not know what her reaction would be. She seemed to consume and absorb herself with the injustice that had been done to her by taking my father away and leaving me in his place, I felt some misgivings about leaving her on her own. She was not an old woman, but my parents had taken so long in conceiving me that she had been almost forty before I jumped into the world. But she had a maid, and a small coterie of women friends of her own age who came to the house and whom she visited. I gathered up my courage one evening and informed her of my intention to marry.

She had complained enough about my absences, about using her house as a dormitory, about my activities, at which she 'could only guess'. Now, to my intense surprise, her face lit up in genuine pleasure.

'Yes – a man should marry young,' she said. It would be the making of me. Who was the girl? Was I serious? Had I considered the gravity of such a step? My responsibilities? It was not simply a wartime romance? I gave her details. She seemed satisfied. Then she began to talk with animation about how we must reorganize the house. Of course we must first of all live here until I had found my feet. I was not to regard her as an encumbrance. It was a large house; the rooms could be reallocated so that we, the happy couple, could have as independent a life as possible. We were far enough from the bombing, thank God, to be safe.

We would not be living here, I said, cutting her short. I had somewhere already. A house? A flat? A flat. So, I had it all arranged; she was to be left, it was no more than she had expected.

'Am I at least to meet the young woman?'

I brought Dorothy to dinner the next night. Mother went out of her way to ignore me and addressed most of her conversation, at first probing, then increasingly confidential, almost conspiratorial, to Dorothy. After dinner my mother said with a smile that she would like to talk to Dorothy alone for a while. 'You would not mind that, my dear, would you?' she said, smiling at Dorothy.

Dorothy came out half an hour later. 'Why, she's nothing at all like you said, Cornelius. She was charming. She told me all about you . . .'

They had come to an accommodation.

Now, at last, preparing to leave my room, I sat and weeded out my boyish life and packed what little I thought I needed for the future. And one of the things I left behind me in that room – that had already left me – was Poetry. I had not noticed. I read through my book again, my eyes straying to the hardly diminished piles of copies in the corner. I went patiently and with an increasing sense of shame and pain through the work I had done since then. It really was, I saw, desperately thin stuff. I had moved away from Auden – after his flight to America his stock had fallen rapidly – and invested in a rather dreary surrealism. I had not managed to get into Tambimuttu's *Poetry London*, but it was typically the sort of stuff that filled his pages – wombs, tombs, and mandrake roots. I rolled up the poems, twisted a rubber band around them and consigned the white tube to the back of a bottom drawer – that small, unlit, unfrequented repository – the world over – of momentary neural responses and huge, unrequited labours of love.

I embarked on a new form of creation. *My more secret work . . .* I was seconded to Wolfson's department to make up lives. The lives; the personalities, occupations, births, marriages, modes of dress, relatives, houses, for men and women whose only contact with me was through the briefing details I was given. I consulted Baedekers, maps, newspapers, church and civil registers, photographs, gossip to manufacture identities, not false, but rather constructed from scraps of reality, for agents who were to be sent back to my country to work against the Germans. A small country, it was essential that their covers were true. It was impressed upon me that many of my compatriots were also informants or quislings. I was proud of my imagined lives. At last I was using my gifts in a way useful to others. There was a sense of high purpose about our work.

Then there was a sudden disbandment of our office. Something had happened. I was not told what had happened. Wolfson, that humorous, handsome scholar, sat grey-faced at his desk one morning; in the afternoon he was gone. I was transferred back to my propaganda work. I regretted this. It seemed frivolous compared with what I had been doing.

But the war was progressing. Our armies invaded Europe.

The bombing had long ceased; only the V-weapons were left to terrify us. They fell indiscriminately on areas which had avoided the bombers, the suburbs that had been spared. I remember going home and seeing a half row of bombed houses like a stage-set. Walls showed pink- and blue-flowered wallpapers, a crooked mirror hung above a fireplace, reflecting the sky. There were pale patches where pictures had hung. In one room a chair stood

three-legged on the last remaining bit of upper floor, its fourth leg
stepping into space.

But yet I had avoided the war, as much else, I thought. I slept
well at nights.

I am at the edge of a field and not at the edge. How it is with
dreams. I am slung in a hammock on an early summer's day inside
my head and what is happening is projected – the amethyst-blue
sky, feathered trees, brown birds – as stars are projected into the
curved roof of a planetarium.

The field is large and grows larger. It is flat, lushly green, and
banks away up to a level and unbroken edge. I feel the sea is
beyond. The sky has one small white cloud high up, in the process
of slow disintegration, like stretched, then torn, cotton wool.

Far away I can hear voices shouting and singing most
pleasantly. The strident music of a calliope. All these sounds at a
distance, but getting nearer.

Then I see that two sets of railway lines are laid in a St
Andrew's cross on the field. I am expecting a train. A man walks
across my line of vision – now I am on a platform or the verandah
of a pavilion looking under a scallop-edge awning. The man is
dressed in a business suit with a watered-silk light-blue waistcoat.
He has a gold watch-chain and a gold-cased watch which he is
consulting in his hand. He has short grey hair under his cap. I
know he is the station-master. I am on the station platform. But
no lines come here. They cross on the field in front of us.

Some people are beginning to come over the rise. They spill
onto the brow of the hill – the field is now curved in a modest
pregnancy. The music is louder. I am intensely interested in these
people. They are still far off, but I can distinguish their clothes.
The women are wearing long dresses of white and cream and

carrying parasols. The men are in white or fawn or beige linen coats and trousers.

The trains come on. A great black red-piped steam engine speeds from the right pulling a train of passenger coaches. As the train travels swiftly towards the meeting of the tracks, a second engine races silently from the left. There is no anxiety as to a crash. The two trains pass through each other and run swiftly and gently and silently away on either side of the station. The carriages flow through each other with no collision other than a slight commingling and confusion of bodies of the men and women who look out of the sky-reflecting windows and patrol transparent corridors. They hold children, bonneted, up into the air, avoiding the smoke which sprawls lazily back from the engine chimneys.

Who are these people? I seem to recognize them from old photographs. They are the peaceful dead of old Europe; our grandparents, some parents. I see them now: the gentleman profiled, a grey top hat tilted rakishly forward, his long straight nose, his cigar held, cherished, revolved in a half turn between his lips. His wife, small, dark, smiling. The children, their skirts flying backwards as they race in the corridors, the stockinged legs, the knickerbockers, the high-collared jackets open, the ribbons streaming back, the arms outstretched, clutching forward to . . . And the other women, and other men, and the men with brandy-snuff on their sleeves – and all, all, most alive, most animated, as they move past. And now the carriages have gone, the rails still humming.

The number of people on the hill has grown. The steam calliope has arrived. Bunting of small triangular pennants, red, blue, yellow, red . . . has been hoisted from tree to tree. There are jugglers and dogs on their hind legs and the steam of cooking rises.

I feel happy. So happy. And this changes to ecstasy when I see, rising slowly from behind the edge of the rise, bobbing their stripes, balloons – minor planets that have been emptied of matter and filled with joyous air. One leans and bobs, then straightens and ascends, the lick of flame underneath it seen like a gash in heaven. Then the basket from which a man, my father, and a woman waved coloured handkerchiefs and their mouths open in little black 'o' shapes to shout a greeting I cannot hear. Then do.

They are shouting that the war is over.

That they are the last happy people.

So, was I happy?

Against the trend of history things conspired to make me so.

Mother considered that I had neglected, even abandoned her. On the contrary, being away from her, I had become quite the dutiful son, visiting two or three times a week.

'Alone in this great house with Germans trying to kill me.'

'I'm sure they did not mean it personally.' The joke was ill-advised. 'Anyway, all that is over and done with.'

'Well – what are you going to do now?' she said icily. 'Your father's money won't keep you forever, you know.' It seemed sometimes that she could read my mind. 'Prices are sky-rocketing all the time. These wretched Socialists . . .'

I did not rise to her bait. She went on after a brief pause: 'This house. The expense of it – I have to bear it all on my own. Not that I mind.'

I said nothing. I knew that she was rich from the sale of my father's business in the boom straight after the end of the war. I had long coveted this house – my old room, indeed – but I knew Mother well enough to know that she would refuse on principle anything I suggested.

'I have been thinking . . .' she said. I busied myself with some letters at my father's old desk. '. . . of selling this house.' I still said nothing. 'Though that might cause complications under your father's will.'

'Umm.'

'Your rights.' She handled the word with a pair of tongs.

'Dear Mama, whatever you want. You know that.'

'And how is Dorothy?' Evidently she had decided something in her mind and it was better to drop the subject.

'Oh, well. Very well.'

'Why does she never come to visit me?'

'I shall have to . . .'

'Oh, don't bother. Don't bother. When she sees fit. Will you please pass me that book from the table? Yes. Thank you.'

Dorothy visited the next day and received Mother's confidence. The house was too big. She had found another to her liking – at least, not excessive dislike – in Clapham. It was a further six months before she moved. She had not been particularly well, and I half expected, half dreaded that she might die as a final admonishment to me. But she lived for another twenty years in that lace-curtained villa with its pale moths flitting in the long, tall-hedged, overgrown garden at evening.

So the house at Hampstead was finally mine. Large, sedate, at the end of a street of similar large houses. The row curved so that, standing at the end of the street, one could see our upper back windows. Perhaps fatally, the room I had occupied since our arrival in England now became my work room, its single bed a day-bed for me to rest from my labours.

And now, for the first time, in the long hard winter of '47, I felt truly content. There was something magical about the snowlight reflected from the garden below, reflected down from our bedroom ceiling onto Dorothy's sleeping face stirring, murmuring as I climbed in beside her after a night stint at my work. At last, I thought, I had discovered what love is for. Such knowledge never leaves us. You will wish it would. For when love is gone, its memory heart-rendingly haunts us. Or, worse, taunts. All thought of my self-loathing, anxiety, night-terrors fell away. Now, now, I could write.

I shut myself off from friends and drink. 'Like Flaubert,' I announced to Dorothy, 'I shall be out when the world rings my doorbell.'

And I was. Six, eight, ten hours a day, I shut myself in the boyish room and wrote my first novel. Coffee, cigarettes, lying on the bed, the floor, speaking to the walls, the sky outside the window, the particular lay of pens and pencils on the desk, the numbering of words, the horror of whisky or any other depressant. All the tics and hoodoos of the writer. The holy prisoner.

It doesn't make the book any better. Of course it was published. It was 'brilliant', 'sensitive', 'a fine début'. You know all this. I knew it was a work of genius. My name walked in the stars. I thought continually of those who were truly great (thank you, Stephen) – and numbered myself among them.

But withal, I was modest. I was given reviewing by the people who had favourably reviewed me. I pronounced from my merited height; a small man standing on a pile of books. Mild praise for those I knew. Warnings as to their future development. Destinations. Deteriorations.

It is time for A— to take a step back, to consider how he can widen these present but not urgent obsessions into a more general statement of the human condition – a more, dare one say, universal statement is required in these times.

Much similar balls. The recently dead deposed. Live minnows and small whales dissected, leaving only their bones on the page. Large whales avoided, or praised inordinately. I was, after all, a part of the literary world now. And broadcasting work. A set of programmes on the state of post-war young writers in my native country. I must visit them. I went to Broadcasting House to discuss the project.

Waiting for the lift to come down, I watched impatiently for the indicator to move from the floor above. At last it did. As I was about to step into the lift, my arm was taken in a firm grip.

'Cornelius – my dear old man. What are you doing in this god-forsaken hole?'

Spencer.

'Look, my office is just up on the next floor. We can take the stairs. You look as if you need a drink. You always look as if you need a drink, come to think of it. How's the book going? Dorothy? Grand girl! Haven't seen you for how long?'

'Years, Spencer. Years.'

'New boy here myself,' he muttered, glancing quickly up and down the corridor as he steered me into his office.

Almost unwillingly our friendship began again. He had been married. Separated. 'Wartime flutter – no odds,' he said. I tried to avoid him, but we seemed to run into each other too often – and too often the meeting ended in a long, long boozy lunch that came inchoately to some sort of end as evening slid into the saloon bars. Then woozily home to Hampstead.

I began to drink freely again. My drinking began as early in the day as I liked. I made it quite early. I imagined that drink somehow enabled me to delve down deeper into myself – no, not that – to rise through the glass, the ice ceiling that limited me to a dark cold pool, into the free cold air above. To find . . . to set flowing . . . What?

My great quintet of novels. *The Conquest of Time*. The piloting of myself, Palinurus-like (thank you, Cyril), through the social and sexual seas, lakes, ponds inhabited by my fellow, contemporary fish; the erecting of card houses; the teaching of parrots to talk; the sexing of mannequins; the mastery of ventriloquism; the hunt for false noses, beards, wigs in the novelist's prop basket; the whole fitting-out and provisioning and transporting of this company of my fictional life exhausted and frequently depressed me.

Throughout my early life I had read hungrily in the lives of great writers, and felt that the tortures of composition they recorded were the ones I now felt. And indeed, writing *drains* one; how susceptible one becomes to minor madnesses. Greed. Jealousy (a curtain drawn back by a hand, a figure stepping out of view, the curtain dropping back into place – do you know that odd story of Mozart, how he was caught in the alley, crouching beneath a window of his own house, listening for the faint, infuriatingly ambiguous sounds of unseen infidelity?).

It was all absurd. I flew out to interview people for my feature on writers in my country. At Mother's request, I made a sentimental diversion to visit our relations in the city where I was born. A senile uncle did not recognize me, but roared in the filthiest language that I was not welcome whoever I was.

The streets were still not healed after the war. The attempts to patch had resulted in modern grotesqueries upsetting the former harmony of water and stone. It was not a good trip. I left for home a day early.

The cab was halted by traffic briefly, preventing it turning into the crescent. I looked out of its window to admire the light of the declining English sun on the back of my house, its rosy, glowing brickwork, the bronze sky reflected from its blue-slate roof . . . The blind was drawn on the spare-room window – my old bedroom.

As a cloud drifted over the sun, the light behind the white blind showed two shadows. I was transfixed. The two embraced, making a two-backed beast with one huge, misshapen head. The taxi jerked forward. There was no doubt in my mind that one of the figures was Dorothy. But the other – the man? Thrusting money into the driver's hand, I hurried across the pavement.

My short strides seemed to take an eternity to reach the steps, to mount them, fumble out my keys, push open the door.

In the hall my distraught face passed swiftly across the mirror. The door to the sitting-room was ajar. I heard a man's voice talking indistinctly. Dorothy's voice replied: 'Of course you don't.'

As I came in, they turned, glasses in their hands. Dorothy with an, 'Oh, Cornelius – you're back early.' Spencer – for of course it was Spencer – greeting me with that large, charming grin that was never surprised. I was surprised. And confused. Had they seen my taxi? Heard me in the street? Surely not in time to dash down here and play this charade?

I went across to the drinks cabinet. I began to pour myself a whisky. My hand was shaking.

'Is there anyone else in the house?' I heard myself ask.

'Anyone else? In the house? No – of course not. What do you mean, Cornelius?'

'Something I heard . . .' I set down my glass, spilling the drink over my hand. 'Excuse me.' I was always polite.

I left the room steadily. But then I ran up the stairs. One flight. Two. Along the landing to the small bedroom. In the muted yellow light that shone through the blind I peered round the room. The single bed was made up, the coconut mat set perhaps too squarely beside it. I went to the bed. The upper sheet and covers were not tucked securely under the mattress as was – surely? – normal. Had I made it? Left it undone? Why should it be as neat as this? I pulled back the covers and knelt to snuffle like a

dog for any trace of sexual odours – the smell of Dorothy's sharp,
thin cologne, the musky scent of Spencer's brilliantine rubbed off
onto the pillow . . . and yes, and no, there was something there
in that too sharp creasing of the bottom sheet that a careful hand
had failed to smooth. Not in what I knew, but in the doubts and
suspicions I could not prove – that way madness lay. I sniffed the
room for any lingering trace of their activity. They had been
unusually clean and tidy lovers. I had not expected such
prissiness, I said to myself descending the stair, from our wild
colonial boy. I saw Dorothy and Spencer below in the hallway.
They were talking in low voices, their heads together, and both
looked up to watch me come down.

I stared straight into Spencer's eyes and he almost impercepti-
bly – or was it a purely nervous gesture? – shrugged his shoulders
as if to say, 'Fair cop, old boy. Fair cop.' He picked up his hat – I
hadn't noticed that – from the hall table and put it on.

Years ago I had admired the flamboyance, the elegant bugger-
you-allness of that hat. Now I said hotly, 'Aren't you a little old
for that absurd hat?' and swept into the sitting-room. To stand by
the window, shaking slightly, my palms sweating.

An energetic mumble of voices came from the hall. It made me
feel momentarily victorious. At last I heard the front door shut.

'You will be glad to know that Spencer has gone,' said my
wife, entering the room angrily. 'What on earth has got into you?'

I marched ridiculously up and down.

'You are mad. You must be,' said Dorothy. Then she heaved
up her shoulders and let out a great sigh. I stopped opposite her.
Tears stood in my eyes. She fiddled with a magazine, flipping the
pages irritably back and forth.

'What . . . ?' But I never asked the question. I studied her thin
mouth, her face turned tensely down. 'What,' I asked in the end,
'did he want anyway?'

'To see you. You weren't here. He had a drink. All right?'

The dangerous point had been passed. I would never again be in such a position.

'Dinner will be in half an hour,' and she left the room.

That night I compounded my cowardice. In bed, as I lay hunched away from her, Dorothy's arm came round me. I shifted away. 'Cornelius,' she whispered. I turned to her . . .

Such compassion I had. Such forgiveness. It is the first time I have talked about this. The first time I have recalled it – for a week at least. And it can still make me cry. Like a piece of music. Let us think of a piece. Ravel's *Pavane pour une infante défunte*. Yes, that has the right, lachrymal quality . . . Perhaps all of life is simply the pre-selection of material which we then, at our leisure, proceed to fuck up.

Suffice it to say that life with Dorothy continued on an outwardly even tenor. My unwillingness to question her meant that she could tell me no lies. I could choose to believe in our day-to-day life. In her innocence. We have to live with such untruths.

I saw Spencer a month later in the Highlander. His hat was on the bar. He pretended not to see me at first, engaged with a group at the bar, but then came over with that same wide smile. 'Long time no see, Cornelius. Have a drink.' To my shame I accepted.

I stood at the edge of the conversation. The group rapidly melted away to their homes, or whatever arrangements they had. Only one was left with us. Spencer began to talk about 'the old days'.

'Charlie,' said Spencer, 'Cornelius here was in Wolfson's lot in the war. Do you remember that?'

Charlie looked at me in a curious, cold way. 'Yes, I do,' he said. 'Bloody disaster. Bloody disgrace.'

'What do you mean?' I said.

'All the agents were taken, weren't they?' said Spencer. 'Some cock-up along the line, according to what I heard.'

'Don't be silly . . .'

'Nothing bloody silly,' said Charlie. 'Excuse me.' He drained his whisky quickly and banged the glass on the bar and walked away.

'What the hell does he mean?' I said.

'Don't worry about it, old boy,' said Spencer. 'Charlie had to mop up. Doesn't like to talk about it. Nothing to do with the likes of you, Cornelius. There was talk about a leak, or some faulty leg-work in the section. Have another.'

'I don't see how anything . . .'

'Two whiskies, please, Maisie.'

I drank it in silence. I left shortly after, making some lame excuse about going on somewhere. Not home.

'See you again, old chap. Ha, ha,' he shouted after me.

It made no difference that I learned later that all of our agents had been expected and taken shortly after landing. I comforted myself that they had been betrayed. Not by me. I was absolved. My fictions had not been tested by torture or death. I was an artist; the filthy world was nothing to do with me.

But later knowledge is no use – when I left the bar that night all innocence had gone.

The Last Thing

'And did you see him again?'

'In the late seventies. He had grown horribly fat and almost entirely bald. I was glad of that. My pleasure distresses me now.'

'Why?'

'When we are near death we should acknowledge our sins and weaknesses. It is no time to think ill of the dead themselves.'

'So Spencer is dead?'

'You do not know him? I thought he was famous. It is two or three years ago now. I went to his funeral. Judith was there. She looked like her mother. She said only the usual polite, meaningless things. I do not think she remembered me. I took part in a memorial broadcast for Spencer on the wireless. He had done great things in drama, you know. For the radio. I don't suppose anybody takes any notice of that sort of thing now.'

'It has been interesting to hear you talk of your early years in such detail. I wonder if we could now move on to the work. The grand scheme, the great architecture of your quintet – was that there from the start?'

'Oh, *that*. That is all fixed by the time we are twenty-one, two, five. The rest is work and fame or obscurity or the one succeeded by the other – the public world. Where the books come from is from the tiny things seemingly trivial to the outsider. In reality it is all love, and lack of love. It is only love. Does that frustrate you? Go away. I want to work.'

. . . and Pritchard shrinks and shrivels in the armchair. His frizzy hair slips, a tattered rug, forward, sliding down his brow. His hands, lifted in a gesture of supplication, dwindle into the dark tubes of his denim jacket. His mouth, caught in the act of uttering some agonizing plea for mercy, is held in that, and the lips melt, run and dissolve.

He is made of rubber, papier-mâché, fish-glue, cheap wood – his pieces, broken down into their constituent elements, float slowly and lugubriously around the room, fusing glumly with and disappearing into the wood of the bookcases, the leathers and cloths and boards of the books, the plastic hood and tungsten

filament of the desk lamp. The very chair he sat in absorbs his hair
for its stuffing, his flesh for its tan covering . . .

He had made Pritchard. He could dismantle, unconstruct him.
Cornelius had needed someone to talk to; had made him human.
He now unmakes him.

And his girl? Is the same to happen to her? No — not the girl.
She shall stay. Soon she will come looking for her lover.

Wait. Wait, whispers Cornelius to his machine.

She is in the room.

She has on a white dress with a delicate blue and yellow wreath
of forget-me-nots and primroses embroidered round her high
collar, and repeated at the cuffs where her slender wrists emerge.
The skirt swirls gently just below her knees as she turns, turns
again, walking about the room. He gets up from the desk and
comes to her side. The last light of evening is on her face. Her hair
is now blue-black, not mouse-brown, and waves back in deep,
natural waves from her slight, shadowed temples.

'Will you not pull the curtains?' she asks.

When he comes back from the windows she has with some sly
backward movements of her fingers unhooked the dress and steps
from it as it falls in a white pool at her feet.

Now she is all shadows. She steps towards him.

He guides her to his youth, to the sofa.

'Helena?'

'Yes.'

Cornelius Marten lies on the sofa. His breathing is shallow. Every
now and then his shut eyelids twitch very slightly. On the desk is a
writing pad with only the words *Every morning my father* written at
the top of the top sheet. Beside the pad are three cassettes in
boxes. The machine, its red light gleaming, turns the fourth tape
with a faint hiss, recording silence.

Venice Declined

'There are other wives,' he insisted. 'Several. And they will be going. Of course, if you don't think it necessary . . .'

'Is any of it *necessary*?'

He sighed and put a hand to his forehead. 'OK. OK. What is that awful noise?'

'They're setting up for the concert in St Mark's tonight.'

'Sounds hellish.'

'They say the Stones might be there.'

'Oh – Ruskin.' He sniggered.

'What?'

'*The Stones of Venice.*'

'That's what I said.' She had never been able to follow these small donnish jokes. 'Anyway, I'm going to see what's happening.'

'Just so long as you don't actually want to inflict the concert on me. I'd have thought we were just a weeny bit old for that kind of thing. Um? Indeed, that the whole thing was a trifle . . .' He stopped himself just in time from saying *passé*, remembering that he had already used it twice that morning, '. . . a trifle *démodé*.'

'Christ, Roger, I sometimes think you were born a little old man.'

'You're not coming into the city with me then?'

She shook her head and picked up the novel she had brought with her on the plane. Another woman with her hair cut in a pudding-bowl fringe and her body in a shapeless dress stared at him from the back cover. It is, he thought, some ghastly sort of freemasonry.

He opened the door. 'Enjoy your day.'

'Don't try walking on the water,' she muttered, but he had gone.

Despite his wife's jibe, Roger Cox, Professor Roger Cox, was only thirty-seven years old. However, along with a number of his contemporaries in the late 1980s, he liked to ape fashions and thought-processes already dead in his grandfather's day.

He was especially proud of the outfit he was wearing. The fawn suit, and cream-coloured waistcoat embroidered with tiny red flowers. The yellow silk cravat, at first allowed, in front of the mirror, to billow out, was now more decently pressed down. All that was needed was a silver-topped cane – but he knew he could never carry that off. He came down into the small reception area and crossed the brown- and white-tiled floor. The black-suited clerk behind the desk glanced up and down again without acknowledging him.

Outside the air was warm and heavy, compressed between the walls of the narrow street. There were few people about. Natives of the city mostly, he judged by their clothes and purposeful way of walking. Over the high roofs came again the violent sound of the loudspeakers in the square, like a roll of collapsing thunder. A flock of pigeons took off and flickered across the blue sky. With a final huge crackling, the noise ceased and the sounds of the city came back. He began his journey.

Rather stylishly, he thought.

Images of Dirk Bogarde in *Death in Venice* came to mind. The moustache – though Roger's was fuller and droopier. The round wire-rimmed spectacles; but behind them his eyes were rather ludicrously magnified. And his body was perhaps not so compact. There was something boyish about his narrow chest and unmuscular arms of which Roger was alternately proud – that he was not like other men – and ashamed.

It really was very warm. He struck away into the back of the city. Girls in light dresses strolled past hand-in-hand with tee-shirted boys. Even grown men, he saw to his disgust, were in jeans and open-necked shirts. An old woman, enveloped from head to toe in black, came rustling up behind him, trying to pass on the narrow pavement. She smiled toothlessly into his face as he stepped aside. How natural she looked, he thought. And, yes, people should have the decency to suit their surroundings. The internationalization of cheap, tawdry clothing was like, yes, like the internationalization of literature through translation. That was why most English free verse read like a bad translation from the Polish. Must remember that. Bring it in somewhere. He nodded, waiting to cross a bridge over which more inadequately clothed flesh tumbled towards him. No doubt heading, with the dirty canals, to the sea and the Lido.

At last he got into quieter streets. He was sweating. Should he stop and have a drink? But he knew that alcohol would only make him sleepy. Entering a small bar, he ordered a Coke. The can was warm, but he was grateful for the sugary balm. He consumed it greedily, his eyes flicking about above the can. But there was no one here to see him drinking the childish fizz.

A few more streets and he stopped again to mop his brow. The paper tissue disintegrated in his sweat. Would it be decent to return to the hotel yet? After he had made all that fuss about exploring the unknown Venice? How wonderful, though, to stretch out in tepid water in the hotel tub. But he couldn't rely on Sarah being out all afternoon, or know when she would be back.

He went on; through narrowing streets, on cobbled pavements, across innumerable small humpbacked bridges, through alleys and arcades, along the disappointingly plain sides of great buildings whose façades cast dull reflections onto murky water. He twisted endlessly this way and that. A church, welcome at first for its cool interior, repelled by its odd, pervasive smell as if he was in the carcass of some giant, dusty moth. The odour of sanctity indeed. He emerged back into the brilliant street, his mouth wrinkling in disgust.

His lecture was to be delivered to Conference tomorrow. He had hoped to drum up a few more lines on this walk. *The Sensuous Servant* – a good title. Seduction, rape, sometimes, of young female domestics. Hypocrisy of nineteenth century. Sex and domesticity. Astonishing source material in Marcus's book. Unusable direct, of course – in a lecture, at least. Could not bring himself to mouth those passages. Quote from Hardy, Meredith, Butler . . . Butler – what an apposite name for his theme. Bring that out. Point it out. Did name subconsciously affect Butler? Housemaid's knee. Chuckle. Must read dirty bits in Marcus again . . .

Then Roger was assailed by a sudden fear. The lecture wasn't, well – a little old-fashioned, was it? For, without doubt, any argument that smacked of old-style, un-deconstructed Eng. Lit. would be immediately eviscerated by someone like Peter Plowman. Particularly *him*. Plowman was a fellow-academic, and editor of *Zeugma*, a critical quarterly of uncompromising unreadability and great influence. Also a hairy lecher. More than once he had caught Sarah looking at Plowman with the dead-eyed, neutral gaze women use to fully evaluate the large, hairy male.

Descending from yet another bridge and following a canal distinguishable from the last dozen or so only by its slightly greater width, he heard again the loud barks and belches of the loudspeakers being tested. Must have come in a circle. He looked at his watch. Twenty to five. A decent time to be out, after all. He hadn't realized he had been walking for so long. Time to stop and mop again. He stood on the steps of the side door of an ancient palazzo. One of the high, narrow double doors was a little way open, the interior shadowy. Probably an apartment block now. Yes, he could see the bell board. No one was likely to take exception to him standing on the steps. Especially as he was dressed, he assured himself, almost like a local. Might have been taking the air of his own steps. He looked patronizingly up and down the street.

'The milord Byron . . .' A voice wheezed out of the shadowed doorway. Or rather, it was as if the dust and shadow themselves had formed a voice, the doorway its mouth, the dark hall a larynx. For a moment the voice shocked him. Should he move on at once? But a sudden surge of Hawaiian shirts on the pavement pressed him up to the top step. 'Excuse me, sirrr . . .' a giraffe woman requested. Followed by a wallowing, elephantine male, a hugely lensed camera dangling at his loins.

Roger, pressed back further, peered in through the doorway. An old man moved forward into a shaft of pale light. The body was short and sturdy; a peasant's. Reddened wings of hair swept back on either side of a liver-spotted bald head. The face was lively, ancient, brown-pink; the eyebrows, thin and arched, looked as if they had been painted on.

'*Inglese* . . . ?'

'Ah . . .'

'Come in. Please to come in.'

The wave of tourists had passed, but Roger let the old man's firm grip of his wrist draw him into the palazzo. The door-catch clicked behind him and the noise of the city was cut instantly off.

Roger stood in an enormous entrance hall. To his right the main doors that must open on the canal were boarded up. The only light came from a broken panel in a closed shutter high in the wall. Lumps of plaster, fallen from the ceiling, starred the tiled floor. A broad staircase went up to a gallery. At one side of the stairs a door was opened. A radio played from in there. The door was shut again.

'You wish to see the palazzo? You have introduction?'

'As a matter of fact – no,' said Roger. This was too ridiculous.

The old man inspected him. 'No matter. Perhaps something else?'

'Pardon? *Pardone?*' Was that correct?

The old man looked puzzled for a moment, then said, 'Please follow.' He made for the staircase.

At least it was cool in here. No harm in humouring the man. Roger followed.

Halfway up the stairs, they stopped.

'Baldacchino,' the old man announced and bowed. 'My name. *Custode.* Janitor.' He cleared his throat and raised his right arm. 'The staircase is very interesting.'

'Yes.'

'The staircase is very old.'

'You said something – did you not – about Byron? Lord Byron – the poet?'

'This was his home,' said the man with great warmth. 'On this staircase he keep a bear. And a . . . a . . . *mastino?*'

'*Mastino?* Ah.' Roger smiled and tried to look as if he too was casting round for the right translation.

'Wrauf, wrauf,' the old man howled. 'Big dog. Two.'

'Ah. Mastiff, perhaps?'

'Like entrance to Inferno, eh?'

'Well, yes.'

'All English lords have stayed here.' He began to toil upwards again, still talking. '*Il barone* Corvo. Englishman. Very poor. Very mad. On this stairs.'

Corvo struck a chord. Minor writer. 1890s. 1910s. Frederick Rolph or something. Rolfe. *Hadrian the Seventh*. No professional mileage.

'Great men. *Poeti*,' said Baldacchino, heaving himself to the top of the stair. He lurched on along the gallery and down the corridor to his left. 'Many rooms are closed. They are private apartments. You understand. The tower is limited.'

What tower?

'Follow. Follow . . .'

Roger felt some unease as they went down the corridor. As if he were intruding. Behind these heavy doors with brass numbers, lives were being led. Lives which did not include him. Where were they going? 'But . . .' He followed to the end of the corridor. The old man held open a door.

'Come.'

A steep, narrow staircase ascended, wooden, uncarpeted, none too clean. The old man's short, red-corduroyed legs began to stomp purposefully up. There was no banister to hold on to. Roger's fingers clutched tentatively at the roughly plastered walls on each side.

A yellow door at the top. 'My rooms,' said Baldacchino, opening the door, as Roger arrived slightly out of breath on the tiny landing. Baldacchino bowed him into the room.

The shutters were half open. A little, dangerous-looking balcony hung over the side alley. In the middle of the small room, lying in an armchair, was a boy aged about seventeen. Roger had time to take in the gelled-back hair, the rather narrow brown eyes, the too large, bow-like mouth. Then he was aware of Baldacchino at his side, gazing up at him, the Madam Butterfly eyebrows arched higher than ever.

'My grandson, Aldo. Aldo, *Signore* . . . ?'

'Cox. Roger Cox.'

'Signor Coax.'

Oh – should he have given his right name? What if they were thieves? Blackmailers? If they followed him back to his hotel? To England? The old man's red trousers in Bicton Avenue. The eyebrows. The louche young man. 'Aldo!' the old man said sharply.

Aldo stood up in a surly sort of way and bowed to Roger. His white tee-shirt had YALE on the front. His blue jeans bulged grotesquely at the groin as if they were stuffed with hard fruit. He walked indolently round the chair and swayed past Roger. As he did so his eyelids fluttered – widened and fluttered in a gross parody of a cruising tart. Roger looked quickly down. Aldo went into the next room. It had a bed. The door swung slowly shut.

'*Una pesca.*' The old man kissed his fingers to the ceiling. '*Una pesca non colta.*'

'I beg your pardon?' Surely he must be dreaming all this?

'Please – sit.' Baldacchino plumped the cushions on the short, sagging sofa. It was like walking on to a Fellini film set. Roger sat down.

'Strega?'

Was this another form of *prego*?

'The tour of the house? Byron?' he reminded the old man.

'The tower is not possible. Not possible to see very much.

Most rooms are occupy. Not possible to see in them without introduction. Invitation. Strega?' A bottle wagged in front of Roger's face. Thieves were hardly likely to give you a drink, were they? He took the glass of straw-coloured liquor. It had been poured to the brim. The taste was cloying. But in a moment it flowed and thickened in his brain. He tipped back more. It did something to ease the tension he had begun to feel. But there was still something he had to get straight.

'Aldo . . .' he began.

'A beautiful boy.' The old man leaned eagerly forward.

'Indeed. But . . .'

'Another drink.' Baldacchino refilled both glasses. Handing Roger's back, he raised his own, making a toast.

'*Poesia.*'

Ah, poetry. How quaint. 'Indeed. Po-easier.' Why not?

'My family,' the old man began portentously. 'My family was in the service of English gentlemen for, what, *due cento*, two hundred years. It is a proud tradition.'

'Indeed. It must be.'

And the old man's English was quite good, despite the usual peculiarities of pronunciation. What the hell – Roger surprised himself by thinking – it was an adventure. Of sorts. More of the gold stuff was poured into his glass.

'Were they – your family – here in the palazzo when Bryon came to live here?'

'My grandfather – great-grandfather – he was his servant.' Baldacchino pointed behind Roger. He turned. Above the door was a small portrait in a heavy gilt frame. An ikon, the absurdly handsome, luminously-eyed poet gazed down at him.

'Given by the milord Byron.'

'My word. An original?'

Might be worth quite a lot. The innate cupidity of the English middle-class rose in Roger.

'Is a family treasure. A hairloom.'

'An heirloom,' Roger murmured in mechanical correction. What precisely had been the great-grandfather's relationship to the poet? He had read of Byron's bisexuality. There might be an article for the *TLS* in this. He drank more Strega.

'Many ladies. Many, many, in this house. This room.'

'Here? Byron's ladies?' Roger giggled. To think of those long-gone bodies writhing and humping among the dingy furniture. A whirl of invisible flesh.

'And . . .' The old man winked, extending the bottle to refill Roger's glass, '. . . boys sometimes. But he was a great poet – *poeta*. A favour for me, *signore* – I have always loved to be able to hear in his own tongue. Please, tell me some.'

'Ah . . .'

'Yes?'

'You see – Byron is not the most studied poet in English. In English Studies. Today.'

'No?' Baldacchino's eyes widened. 'The most magnificent . . . You do not know his poetry?'

'I'm afraid – very little.' Roger tried a smile.

'Who then do you study?' Baldacchino asked suspiciously.

'Coleridge. Wordsworth . . .'

'Wordswot?' He shook his head.

'My own speciality is the later, rather than early, nineteenth century . . . Meredith. Arnold.'

'Meredit? Arnold?' Baldacchino was bewildered.

'Things have changed a *little* since Byron's day.'

Baldacchino leaned forward. A gold-green genie shimmered in the bottle. 'People, *signore*. People change. Not things. Things do not change. You will find that. Poetry is Beauty.'

Truth. Truth – Beauty.

'Is not so?'

Roger wriggled. 'I think we could say . . .'

'My family for two centuries has served Beauty.' The old man was radiantly alive in a shaft of sunlight. 'Beauty – and the English. I myself serve *il barone* Corvo.'

'Rolfe?'

'Eh? We find him living on the staircase when the palazzo is shut for the winter. He say he has been thrown from his apartment. He will stay on the charity of Byron, he say.'

'How amazing. When was this?'

'I was thirteen years old. Now I am eighty-six. I am a grandfather. Then I was a beautiful boy. He was *gran pederasta*. That is what the English like, eh?'

The old bugger. 'Most certainly not,' said Roger.

The sun went in. The old man sipped at his Strega. 'Not many come here now – but that is what they want.'

'What?'

The old man laughed. 'Beauty,' he said.

Beauty. Truth. Beauty. Roger could feel the inside of his head ascend – an alcoholic lift.

'Not many come.' Baldacchino's moods came and went with the sun in the room. 'The gentlemen are not as they were,' he intoned sadly.

Only a foreigner could use that word now. Gentlemen. It was stepping back in time seventy years. The streets full of men in linen suits. The women wasp-waisted in long dresses. He eased the trouser-creases on his knees. Sarah would never believe him about this afternoon. He saw the smile that was nothing but a wavy, smirking line between her long lips. 'But why ever did you go in . . . ?' she would ask. He was brave and reckless. He was a fool. Byron looked down.

'Margarita,' said Baldacchino.

Oh God — another bottle? But the old man was looking past him. A girl had come into the room from the landing. Roger got up from the sofa. She stood beside Baldacchino's chair and her large, unblinking eyes looked Roger over. She was younger than the boy, say fifteen or sixteen. A sallow, rather disagreeable, pretty face. Body thin, but not weak. The same big bow mouth. A girl in a cheap, skimpy dress. He blushed.

'. . . Coax.' Baldacchino was introducing him. 'My grand-daughter, Margarita.'

The girl smiled. That could mean nothing. The old man motioned her away. She went round the sofa, without looking again at Roger, and through the other bedroom door. The door shut after her.

Now, surely, nothing could happen. Not with the girl here. Perhaps he had read all the signals wrongly. What if all the clichéd oddities of Italian life were true? He drank the rest of his glass. But a feeling of discomfort grew in him. A magnetic field had sprung across the room between the two doors. As if he was an incestuous intermediary between brother and sister. He put his glass on the floor and got to his feet.

Baldacchino was out of his chair with surprising speed.

'You are ready, *signore*?'

'I really must . . .'

'Sh . . .' The old man put a finger to his lips and tiptoed to the boy's door. Slowly turning the knob, he looked back over his shoulder, his face a mask of cajoling invitation, his forehead in brown furrows above the great hoops of eyebrows. The sun going in made his sparse hair seem darker and thicker. He opened the door gracefully — a man drawing back the curtain on a stage.

Aldo, standing, turned to face them. Naked, he ceased to be Aldo. Roger's eyes were seized at once by the sight of the

enormous dangling *thing*, like some giant purple root or bulb –
narcissus, onion . . .

'Argargle – no. No. Please shut the door.'

The monstrous image burned behind his eyes still. The Strega
made the room oddly angled. The re-emerging sun let the table's
varnished top glow like barley sugar.

Baldacchino came in front of him, looking up with concern.
Thank God, Aldo's door was closed now.

'Something is wrong, *signore*?' said Baldacchino. 'You are not
well? *Scusi!* I understand.' He clapped a hand to his forehead. 'I
understand,' he murmured. He knocked firmly on the other
door. 'It is fortunate we have a choice. Margarita?' he called, and
knocked again.

The door opened. It was almost a shock to see the girl dressed.
She stood at the foot of the bed, her right hand resting on one of
the turned posts.

'A smile for our guest,' said the old man. Then something,
chidingly, in Italian. Above the quick smile that she produced, her
brown eyes stared without expression at Roger. The old man
muttered something more, furiously . . . But Roger was already
backing to the safety of the stairs door. The girl sat down on the
bed. She yawned.

'No – no. Really,' Roger said as Baldacchino followed him
across the room.

The old man stopped.

'Neither?' he said. He began to laugh, showing yellow, horse-
like teeth. Margarita allowed herself to look out at Roger. Then
she began to laugh too. Before the other door could open and
Aldo join in, Roger made his escape. On to the tiny landing.
Down the narrow staircase. And soon, walking hurriedly,
imaginary cane hoisted to ward off pursuers, his shoes clacked on
the wooden tiles past all the closed, silent, apartment doors.

Even with the windows shut and the curtains drawn the noise, like constant thunder, rolled into the room. Sarah was painting lotion on her legs. She had, she said, been bitten by mosquitoes.

At last she laid aside the little brush and recapped the pink bottle. 'It looks bloody awful,' she said. 'I shall have to go in my jeans.'

She glanced across at Roger. He was huddled over a tiny table, from which his lecture notes kept trying to slither to the floor.

'Will they serve me?' she asked. There was no response from Roger. 'They must. Hundreds of women dress in them. Jeans or trousers. Roger – are you going to be ready?'

Why had the girl looked at him like that? Roger wondered. He was not repulsive. Some women, he believed, found him quite attractive. Why, in the past, there was Rachel. Lizzie Denton. Jane. That girl at college . . . He fingered his moustache, mourning the women scattered thinly across his youth. And found himself looking at his wife. She had stopped that obscene leg painting. She was asking him something. Was he going to be ready?

'I must finish this first.'

'You can do that in the morning,' said Sarah. 'I said we'd meet Plowman at nine.'

'Yes. Yes.' He had had an hour's sleep after returning, and now felt a little hungover. He could do with a drink.

She went into the bathroom. Was that cheering he could hear? He scrabbled his papers together, retrieving the fallen sheets from the carpet. He couldn't concentrate with that nonsense in the Square. Sarah had left the bathroom door ajar. It was disturbing. Would it swing open of its own accord and reveal Sarah . . . Doing what? With the admirable and slightly repellent openness of their marriage they had few secrets from each other. Even if he didn't like wearing only the trousers of his pyjamas in summer as she had bullied him into doing. His white and hairless chest looked like a haddock. Still, better than wearing the jacket only, when his legs looked as if they were dangling thin and white. A marionette's. Like that story by Kleist about marionettes. Very good, Kleist. Must read him. And move those magazines from behind the poetry shelves. Still, Sarah never read poetry; she would not discover them. A professional thing, poetry. *Poesia*. Byron. The girl Margarita began to slowly raise the black dress . . .

After dinner with Plowman and his Cambridge woman, Diana, Roger treated them all to Strega.

'Don't think I have before . . .' said Plowman, raising his glass, peering quizzically through it at the candle.

'Something I discovered this afternoon. Or, rather, that discovered me,' said Roger modestly.

'Ah.' Plowman nosed the glass, then swallowed some. 'How extraordinary,' he said.

The women lifted their drinks, sipped, and made wry faces after Plowman's, as they put down their glasses. They seemed on the edge of laughter at what had become a solemn, comic ritual. All were silent for a moment, then Sarah spoke up.

'Where did you go this afternoon, Roger?' she asked. 'He's being very mysterious about it.'

The Strega mixing with the Barolo they had drunk made Roger feel warm and secure, in the possession of secrets it might possibly be amusing to tell.

'I had such – a rather peculiar – adventure this afternoon.'

'Adventure? Adventure – you?' Sarah laughed. 'Sorry. It just sounded funny. Sorry.' She straightened her face and tried to look very serious. And laughed again.

'God,' said Plowman. 'This is like an opening to Conrad or something. All gathered on the deck of a boat. Narrative within narrative. Isn't there one that begins like that? Intrigue us, Roger. Intrigue us.' He laughed too, and took advantage of his merry moment to slide an arm across the back of Diana's chair. His hand dangled over her shoulder.

This mockery made Roger less sure of his reception, but he went on and told them of his adventure. He knew his face was on fire before the end. Trying to make the old man amusing, he made him sound only mad.

'Byron?' said Plowman. 'Who remembers Byron?'

'The Byron of *Don Juan*. *Bembo*,' Roger pleaded in exoneration.

'*Beppo*,' Diana corrected him. She wore Plowman's hand on her breast like a newly awarded decoration.

'And who's this Corvo character?' Plowman pursued him.

'Fringe figure . . . my period,' Roger mumbled.

'Ah. One of your lot.' Plowman was Modern American Studies.

'Listen. You haven't told us.' Sarah's face glowed in the candlelight. Her eyes sparkled. 'Which one you chose. The boy or the girl?'

The atmosphere round the table was one of barely suppressed laughter, ready to boil out and swamp him if he made the wrong answer. What was the right answer?

'Come on.' Plowman was lighting one of his little cigars.

'Well, none of them. Neither,' Roger stammered.

'Neither?'

'Of course not.'

'Oh, what a swiz,' said Diana.

'Think they were having you on a bit there, Roger.' Plowman blew foul smoke before him. His hand now gripped Diana's bare shoulder. 'How's the lecture? All ready for tomorrow, are you?' he asked, with a smirk. Roger's story had been dismissed.

'Shouldn't go gallivanting off like that before the great day, you know.'

Oh yes, ready for tomorrow, Roger thought. And tomorrow. And tomorrow. Oh bloody, miserable, exacting life. Why couldn't it shove off for a bit?

Sarah was still gazing at him, a peculiar smug victory on her face.

Which one would you have chosen? her look asked. And how long would it be before she actually asked that question? On what awful, intimate occasion?

The Monocle of My Uncle

He would take a piece of paper and with rapid scratches of fine pencil, out of a thicket of grey twists and spikes, scribbles and cross-hatchings, make suddenly appear a man riding a bicycle, the front wheel twisting sideways, its spokes instantly dashed in by the pencil point, the man about to fall over the handlebars.

A very funny drawing – no matter how many times I asked him, Uncle Rex would repeat it.

'You've got violinist's hands,' his father's part-time gardener had said, as boy-Uncle Rex twisted the last plum from a wizened tree . . . So Rex told me, laughing.

But he was very proud of the beautifully formed nails, the delicately graceful backward bow of the fingers when he tensed them. I remember him sitting by the open window of his room, his hands laid lightly on his grey flannel trousers; as he yawned and stretched, his fingers splayed slowly out like a cat's exquisite claws.

That was when he flattered me by explaining that children are more intelligent than adults because their bodies are at one with their minds.

'There is,' he said, 'no tug to tear them apart.' He leaned forward and flicked elegantly a dead blue-bottle from the white-painted window-ledge. 'You do not know what I mean,' he added sadly.

He took off his glasses and cleaned one of the lenses vigorously with a tissue. When he replaced them and looked at me again, he blushed.

My father was a Captain in the Army and that year, 1965, he was in Aden. In our white concrete bungalow, one November Sunday afternoon, my mother sat addressing Christmas cards to people back home. My father sipped a beer. I was reading in a corner.

'Do you think this will do for Rex?' she asked my father.

He peered at the card she held up. His shirt was stained with sweat under the arms.

'How should I know?' He rubbed his nose energetically. 'But I shouldn't think so. Bit simple for him, isn't it – robins and things?'

She turned it to her again and looked disappointed.

'Oh, do you think so? It's so difficult. And I don't know what to buy him.'

'A book. Lots of books. Anything like that. Poetry.' He coughed, as if something had stuck in his throat.

'Poetry. How peculiar.'

My father's face coloured for his brother. 'He's always liked that sort of thing. Or art. They're bound to have something in one of the wog shops. Try Shamsuddin's.'

'Um.' She wrote something against Uncle Rex's name on her list.

Later that evening, as he turned off the local Forces network production of *Night Must Fall*, my father returned to the subject.

'That was really quite good, wasn't it? There are a couple of poofters help run a show on there – they'll know what's the thing.'

'What thing?'

'For old Rex's present. Poetry book. I'll ask them what they recommend.' He lapsed into silence, sucking at his pipe.

'Well,' said my mother eagerly, 'who are they?'

'Who?'

'They – you know – the poofters.' Gossip was prized in this small community.

'Oh, couldn't possibly tell you that.' He laughed. Then he said worriedly, 'You don't think, if I do ask them, that they'll think I'm – well – making advances . . . ?'

In the New Year I came back to England. I was a boarder at a school on the soft southern edge of the Midlands. The school had been chosen because it was only a few miles from where my grandparents lived. Of course, I meant to go and see them every weekend, but it was a Saturday in early May before I cycled over to their village.

I had hoped Rex would be there. He was ten years younger than my father and I had always thought of Rex as belonging to me rather than the grown-up world.

'I'm afraid your uncle is away in London this weekend, but I'm sure he wouldn't mind you using his room,' said my grandmother over tea.

Staying out was not allowed, I explained. 'I must really be getting back soon.'

Before I left, I went to the bathroom. I met my grandfather at the foot of the stairs. 'All right, Paul?' he asked. 'Don't tell your grandma.' He pointed down to the mud-encrusted wellingtons. 'Back to the garden,' he whispered.

'I shall have to go soon . . .'

But he was already walking gingerly across the hall, past the open living-room door.

The flushing cistern still reverberated in the bathroom. The landing was lined chest-high with overspill bookshelves. I stood in Rex's doorway. The room was long, narrowly rectangular. A single bed, made up with a pink and white counterpane and one white pillow. The walls were painted white and the whole room had a plain, monastic air – until you looked at the pictures on the wall: reproductions and larger posters, and one or two of his own drawings; of the room itself, his self-portrait framed in a mirror . . .

One picture I loved: a tall, blue, thundery sky; a dark-green forest edge that hung like a wave over the small, lonely figure of a shepherd who leaned on a staff and stared mysteriously out of the picture.

'Giorgione,' said Rex. On my next visit he was back, showing me his room. I was fourteen – it seemed absurd to call him Uncle any longer.

'And that one there?'

A host of black-overcoated, bowler-hatted businessmen hovered on the house faces and over the roofs of a street of suburban villas.

'What are they doing? Coming down or going up?'

'It's hard to tell. You don't know if they're ascending to heaven or raining down. Or perhaps simply suspended there.'

Two women, attended by a dwarf, two doves and a peacock, played with two small, fierce-faced terriers on a roof-top.

'*Two Courtesans on a Balcony*.' He peered at the picture. 'I don't suppose you know what a courtesan is?'

'Yes . . . What?'

'Eh? Oh – a tart. You know.'

I looked away at his books. There were hundreds in the case that ran along the wall opposite his bed – poetry, novels, and the large, expensive art books he collected. There was a desk by the window. And through the window just then came an extraordinary noise from the garden below. Rex leaned on the window-ledge and looked down. I went and stood beside him.

Through the front garden gate, making the cackling and honking sounds we had heard, waddled two large, ugly birds, the size of small turkeys. Idly and arrogantly they strutted, gaining the short, smooth grass of the lawn. Their heads were crowned with grey-pink, misshapen combs that looked like deformed, perhaps venereally diseased, foreskins.

They made again their irritable, mocking calls.

'Guinea-fowl,' said Rex. 'They come from the cottage across the road. I shall have to go and shoo them out, I suppose.'

But the window of the living-room below was suddenly opened and my grandmother yelled, 'Frank, Frank. Those horrible birds are here again.'

In a moment my grandfather came lurching round the corner of the house. He saw us looking down.

'Damn things,' he shouted. He pointed to the birds. They ignored him. He began to wave his arms about as he advanced on them. Unhurriedly they moved towards the gate and slowly, halting in the middle of the road for a final contemptuous ruffling display, they made their way back to the garden across the road.

I glanced up, smiling, at Rex. His face flushed, he grinned and his hand scattered my hair with an odd, brusque motion.

I grew up early, flying alone to and from Aden, and then Cyprus, in the long vacations of summer and Christmas. Then my parents returned to England and my father announced that he was leaving the Army while he was still young enough to do something else. The something else was a job as Personnel Officer at the Coventry headquarters of an engineering firm. When I opened the letter informing me that my exam results were only average, ruling out University, my father took charge. 'The best thing you can do,' he said, 'would be to apply for one of the management trainee openings at the firm. Now.'

But I couldn't join the scheme until I was eighteen. The best part of a year was mine.

We moved into the suburbs of Coventry. The house next to ours was called The Laurels.

'You should call yours the Hardys,' said Rex.

'Oh yeah. Yeah.' I groaned and turned my mouth down in the way we had done at school at a bad joke.

Rex looked disappointed, then he shrugged his shoulders and grinned. 'Laurel, Hardy. Hardy, Laurel. Hum.'

We had driven over one Sunday. When we pulled up outside the gate Rex stepped out to greet us. He looked smaller than I remembered. When I got out of the car he joked about how I had grown; I was now a couple of inches the taller. He shook hands solemnly with me.

My grandparents were in the living-room. In all the greetings and laughter, the settling into chairs, the start of eager conversation, I looked round for Rex. He wasn't there and did not appear.

I edged out and went upstairs.

He was at his window, hands folded behind his back, looking out.

'I wish I had a room like this.'

He turned. 'Oh, I don't live here any more. I'm just "up here on a visit", as it were.'

I wondered why he made that sentence sound so affected, so ironically self-protective.

I saw that the bookcases had been half emptied, most of the pictures stripped from the walls.

'Do you still draw things?'

'Not very often.' He no longer belonged in the room himself.

'Could I see them – your drawings?'

'They're not here, I'm afraid. London. In London.'

'Paul.' My mother's voice came up the stairwell. 'We're taking tea in the garden. Is Rex with you?'

I answered, standing in the doorway. We heard them going out, clanking and clinking. 'I suppose we have to,' I said. He made no attempt to move. 'Coming down?'

'In a moment.'

We sat in striped canvas garden chairs. Rex was on the outer edge of the wide lawn, in the shade of one of the lilac trees, its plump bunches of little flowers starting to brown. I got up and walked over to him.

'I could come round and see you in London if I ever get down there, couldn't I?' I asked.

'Any time, Paul. Any time.'

The time was not until a couple of years later.

I had to go down to London for an interview. This was in the seventies, of course, when jobs were easy to come by. 'Your uncle will put you up,' said my father rather grumpily. He didn't want me moving away from the Company, or home. 'You'd better ring first.'

I hardly recognized Rex's voice when I rang. He would be delighted to see me. I went down by train a week later.

He lived in a quiet, tucked-away little cul-de-sac on the edge of Brixton. It was early evening when I got there; my interview was the next day.

I walked down the street of small Victorian terraced houses. One or two had been gentrified and the inevitable Citroën stood outside; by others battered vans sagged into the kerb. At the house before Rex's number an old, bald man leaned on the front gate.

'Do you want Rawlings?' he asked loudly as I went past.

'Pardon? No.' Our family name was Graham.

'Because they've all gone out. They've left me all on me pissin' own.'

'Oh.' I went on to Rex's gate.

'Do you know what the dirty buggers did?' the mad old man shouted. 'Do you know . . .'

I went down the side of Rex's house.

'You're not Rawlings, are you?' I asked jokingly as he led me into his living-room.

'Rawlings?'

'Something the old man next door said.'

'No.' He laughed. 'He's Rawlings. The poor old thing's a bit senile, I'm afraid. Don't put your bag there.'

He removed it from the long white leather sofa. On the table in front of the sofa were gin, vermouth, lime-juice bottles and two glasses.

'That's better.' He smoothed a disturbed cushion. 'Sorry – one gets rather pernickety. Now, do sit down. Would you like a drink?'

'No, thanks. I don't all that much.'

'What? I do, I'm afraid.' He began to pour himself one. 'Well, how are you?' He raised the glass, staring at me over it.

'Fine.'

There was a difference in him. On his own ground he was far more assertive and confident, perhaps too much so. But the biggest change – I don't know whether to call it an addition or a subtraction – was the appearance of a shockingly deep scar all the way down his right cheek. It looked as if the skin had been slit to the bone, the two sides of the cut held apart, then folded in to each other to make a ridged valley. I tried to avoid looking at it.

'I'm cooking up a sort of bolognese for dinner,' he said.

While he was in the kitchen I looked round the room. Again, books and pictures – above the fireplace, a large framed sketch of a sleeping boy, drawn in heavy charcoal strokes on blue paper. It did not look Rex's style at all.

'Yours?' I asked, when he came back in.

'No. Wish it was.'

We drank red wine over dinner. The light drew away and he cleared the plates with the room in near darkness. When he returned from the kitchen he switched on the lamp in the corner and poured himself another large gin, with a little of the lime juice added.

'It's called a gimlet,' he explained.

I felt restless and a bit bored. 'Don't you ever feel lonely? On your own in this house?' I asked.

He swirled the drink slowly in his fist, gazing into it. 'I'm not always lonely.' He sipped, now looking at me over the glass. Then he turned away and drank the rest in one go and set the glass down sharply. 'Well,' he said, 'there's always the telly. There's a film on. *Red River*. I was going to watch it if you didn't turn up. Do you want to see it?'

We sat at opposite ends of the sofa and watched the tremendous riverside fight between John Wayne and Montgomery Clift.

I didn't ask Rex any more questions about his life. I knew that my father regarded his brother nowadays with a mixture of exasperation and amusement.

When I had asked him if Rex sold his drawings and paintings, my father laughed.

'Hardly. He has to work for a living.'

'What does he do?'

'Works in one of the big stores down there. Selfridge's. Window-dresser or something.'

'Floor Design Manager,' said my mother. 'Get it right. He really is very clever.'

I stirred at the end of the film and looked at Rex. His spectacle lenses reflected the light and hid his eyes. He smiled. The scar stretched white-red on his pale face.

I yawned ostentatiously.

'I'll show you your room.'

The spare bedroom was as neat and tidy as the rest of the house. It looked utterly unused. He asked me what time I would like calling.

When he had gone downstairs again I heard him put on some music quietly; something classical I didn't know; a flute and harp; the clink of glass and bottle . . .

In the morning he got breakfast, telling me the times of buses into the city, giving me directions – then dismissing the idea of them and insisting that I must have a taxi. He seemed to be trying to make amends for the rather cold and unsuccessful evening before.

'The best of luck, Paul,' he said when the cab came. 'You're going straight back?' I think he was rather relieved that I wasn't staying for another night. 'Let me know how you go on. My love to Roger and Gwen.'

He stood in the pathway and waved. I felt embarrassed, but the cab-driver pushed open the onside passenger door and waited without interest for me to enter.

I didn't take the job in London: I wasn't offered it. And I didn't see Rex again until the day of my wedding.

Anna came from the next village to where my grandmother now lived alone – my grandfather had died the winter before. I'd met Anna on one of my visits; I had a car and came over three or four times a week, sometimes staying the night at Anna's, sometimes with my grandmother.

Anyway, I'd invited Rex and he was staying at the old house. The morning of the wedding my father and I drove over to pick them up.

I sat in the back with my grandmother and Rex in the front with my father. All the way, she kept looking at Rex's cheek, and then looking away. I don't know what he'd told her about how he'd got the scar. And all the way, Rex made nervous, facetious comments about my living to regret this day, quoting Byron and Samuel Johnson on the inadvisability of marrying.

'For God's sake shut up, Rex,' my father said roughly. 'What do you know about it, anyway?'

When we got to the church, Rex fell away – or I no longer noticed him. The guests at your own wedding are Others, all suddenly relegated to the past.

The reception was held in the Parish Hall.

'How bucolic,' Rex said, once more at my shoulder as we went in.

Anna was borne off in a swell of relatives and friends and I stood at the bar between Rex and my beefy new brother-in-law. Rex ordered pints for us, and a large gin for himself.

The afternoon ran away rapidly and happily. Anna and I were

not going away until the next day and, after an hour back at my grandmother's when we changed, we rejoined the party at the hall. I had not had much to drink, carrying the same pint glass in my fist for half the evening.

The hall was opposite the village pub and as the light began to fail people came from over there and it became a public dance. The tables were cleared and folded back against the wall.

I don't know whether you have been to any of those village dances. They're dying out pretty quickly now, but that one can't really have changed much since the sort of thing described in Thomas Hardy. The fiddles and cornets might have given way to this loud, amateurish discothèque, but the same mix of eight- to eighty-year-olds was there. The same drunks hugged the bar, the same farmers' sons went galumphing wildly up the centre of the long wooden floor, dragging their girls behind them with great jumping steps of their own invention.

It was about half-past eleven when my father gripped my elbow.

'We're not going yet, old chap, but I thought I'd warn you that we'll be pushing off soon.' He smiled 'OK?'

'Yes. Thanks.'

'Where's Rex? Have you seen him? He's supposed to be with us. I hope he's not pissed.' Irritation clouded his face. He scanned the room.

'Give me the keys. I'll get the car.'

'No, no. I will.'

'I need the air.'

He smiled again and handed the keys to me. 'If you want to go off now, we can get a taxi.'

'Don't be silly, we'll give you a lift,' said Anna's mother, putting her hat, slightly awry, between us.

'Back in a moment.'

From the door I took a last look at that room, a boozy, smoky paradise, and stepped outside.

The sky was blue-black, beginning to cloud around the moon. Across the way a single light shone in the closed pub. I went down the shallow steps to the yard, half full of glistening, silent cars.

From along the shadowed blind side of the hall came an odd sound. At first I thought it was pair of lovers; a gasping; a scuffle; but then a dull thud. Another. The lump of bodies at the wall broke into three shapes – one sitting against the wall, two men standing away. They scraped their shoes on the gravel and walked casually towards me, passing me on either side.

'I should get him out of here,' said the older one. He was about forty-five, with a few hairs plastered over a broad bald head. The other, in his early twenties, red-faced under a mat of coarse curly hair, grinned. 'Poof,' he said in explanation, nodding back at the figure against the wall. They went back inside.

The man at the wall, now struggling to get up, was Rex. When he came forward the solitary brilliant floodlight at the corner of the yard made his face vivid. From his bottom lip a thin, dark slug of blood hung. He wiped it with his sleeve, smearing it across his chin.

'Hello, Paul,' he said, and limped towards me. One lens of his glasses had been shattered into a star.

Reaching into his suit pocket he brought out a packet of cigarettes and put one between his lips. His hands trembled, but he tried to do it with style. 'Ran into a spot of trouble. Have you got a light?'

He removed the cigarette from his mouth. The end was dark. I patted my pockets automatically for non-existent matches.

'I'm sorry, I don't,' I said ridiculously.

He sat in the back of the car and pretended to be drunker than he was when the others got in.

My father said, 'Rex, what on earth have you done to yourself?'

Rex put a hand to his mouth.

'He fell over,' I said.

When we arrived back at the house he got out quickly, but the light in the porch caught him and my grandmother, opening the door, wailed. 'Oh, Rex. On a day like this. You've spoiled everything.'

He came to our first christening. His face had filled out but the scar was still horribly prominent. I felt most important and spoilt as people complimented me on my son. I was rather patronizing to Rex.

'You must be his godfather, Rex. And when he's old enough you must do him your famous drawing.'

'What drawing?'

'You know. The man on his bike. Falling off.'

At first I thought he didn't remember but then he looked at me with a real hatred in his eyes.

'That was for you,' he said. 'No one else. For you.'

Cherry Vodka

In the flat below her were a young couple who made no noise. Along the corridor was a man who said he had been a Member of Parliament. She kept thinking he had died; she would not see him for months on end and then he would half appear again, his back going into his flat, his fallen purple face peering into the dark corridor, his door held a little way open as she passed.

Her own flat was almost too expensive but she was in love with a part of it. There wasn't much to love. The bathroom was so small that the door banged against the bath, and the bath had its taps right up against the wall so that you grazed your knuckles turning them. The kitchen was no more than a curtained-off alcove. A small, square bedroom. But the living-room flowered out – through a narrow arch she could step into a seven-sided, five-windowed turret that hung like a barrel on the north angle of the Edwardian house. From there she could see, between the roofs, a green wedge of Hampstead Heath.

She worked in there. She sat at a small table with one pile of exercise books on her right diminishing, one on her left mounting. When she had finished marking she picked up the letter from her brother, James, and read it again.

For every four or five letters she sent, he returned one reply. He was in what he continued, to annoy her, to call Rhodesia. She read quickly through three pages of large, sprawling handwriting. Always the same: cheerful, with news of people in places she had never heard of; money, horse-riding, his plans. *I'll be leaving soon*, he wrote, *but there are problems getting money out.*

He enclosed a snap of the boy, Michael, thin-legged and brown, his arm round the shoulders of a black boy. They stood in front of a long, sloped horizon, a blue, surprisingly English sky flagged with white clouds. On the back of the photograph James had written *Before the Election* and followed it with two large exclamation marks. *Come over*, he had written in the days of Smith and the white take-over. *Do come.* But she would not. 'I will not go,' she had said sharply to the empty room. It was bad then; her brother was wrong. In a place like that you could only either acquiesce and be tolerated, or protest and be hated.

His invitation had come on a postcard. The picture was presumably an added enticement – the main street of Salisbury; a purple tree and the blue glass and white walls of a bank; the concrete immaculately white, the grass and sky too vividly green as in an hallucination.

'They are living in a dream and will not wake up,' she had said to Mouter, the deputy head at the school where she taught.

'Well, I certainly wouldn't go there,' said Mouter. 'Even considering they'd ever let me in. End up in jail in a month. Wouldn't be able to keep my mouth shut.'

A man she disliked, in his early thirties, unmarried, balding, the stink of tobacco on his clothes – but the only one in the staffroom she could talk to, wished to talk to, the only one with the faintest intelligence.

And intelligence was a quality she enjoyed in herself and rarely in others. Not from any sense of pride. But sometimes she simply knew that she had somewhere opened a wrong door and stepped through, and in the world in which she seemed to find herself what she held was rare and to be clutched on to . . .

The holiday stretched ahead of her. She was not going anywhere this year. Last year had been Greece; next year, she hoped, it would be Russia. And she was going to learn the language. Properly – a pure new study.

Before the summer break she had started on the Penguin course. She had found the language simple at first. How starkly nouns stood – bridge, desk, chair, house – in their transparent land. She borrowed a record from the library and was surprised to hear how liquid and malleable the vowels sounded; she mimed and murmured to the odd, bubbling vowels and soft, butting plosives. She had realized it was necessary to find someone to talk with. When she took back the record the library gave her the name of a woman to contact. A Mrs Nowak. On the edge of Camden Town. She felt like a student again.

She left the photograph of the two boys propped on the desk. She wrote to Mrs Nowak. From then on, on Fridays she read her Russian grammar, walked in the open catacombs of Highgate Cemetery, and on Saturdays she went to Mrs Nowak.

She looked round. The man hesitated in the doorway and went to withdraw apologetically. 'Ah, here is Stefan,' Mrs Nowak sang out.

Miss Granger, on her third visit, had not met the husband before. Half rising from her chair, she touched the palm of the held-out hand with her fingertips.

'I am very pleased to meet you,' he said. 'Halina looks forward so much to you coming – she says you make her feel like a teacher again. Halina?'

His wife had produced a five-pound note from the purse on the table. He took the note and tiptoed gravely out, giving a little bow as he went.

Mrs Nowak closed the book in front of her. 'That is Stefan before the war.' She pointed to a framed photograph, in the grey-gold tinting of the thirties, that stood on the mantelshelf.

'He was training to be an accountant but of course the war interrupted all that. When we came to England, you know, after the war, he was not qualified for here. We were not qualified for anything! I felt so stupid. We could not speak very much English and first we went to Birmingham. Oh, and we thought the people there so cold and hard. It was not at all like the England we read about in books back home. You know, Miss Granger,' Mrs Nowak said – with a sudden slide from buoyancy to gravity, her brow wrinkled up and she shook her head slowly from side to side – 'they were not friendly. When I went into the shops they could not understand what I wanted and I had to stand and stand about until they had served all the others. Everybody before me. I am sure they swindled us all the time on rations. Do you remember? Sometime I will have to show you all the photographs I have.'

'That would be lovely. But look, I must go.' She wasn't sure that she liked being co-opted into Mrs Nowak's past – she had only been ten at the war's end, after all. It was nearly four. The lesson was an hour long. 'Thank you very much. That was most pleasant.'

The end of the lesson had fallen quickly into this pattern: the two copies of Turgenev's *Fathers and Children*, which Miss Granger had chosen, and with which Mrs Nowak was bored, were closed; for almost an hour Mrs Nowak had read from her copy one slow sentence at a time, her spectacles magnifying the spotted lids of her eyes – to be followed by a murmured response – a frown for the incorrect, a smile for the achieved pronunciation. Then Mrs Nowak would make tea and, leaning back in her chair, bring her life back into that small room crowded with heavy, dark furniture.

The photographs were shown, in careful selections. Mrs Nowak as a girl. With dog. With brother. With half of father's face, half nose, half teeth in smile close up. At a table full of glasses and bottles, overlooking a sepia Lake Como. Soldiers smiling, with Mrs Nowak in the middle, huge-breasted, amiable, massed in a uniform. The Pyramids; a camel; Rome; Stefan and a huge, kilted Scot.

'And this is the church at home . . .' Mrs Nowak dealt another picture on to the heap in front of Miss Granger.

'We lived in the East. People don't remember that when the Germans invaded from the West, the Russians came from the East. Here is the town where I lived.'

Mrs Nowak paused while the picture was studied.

'Pinsk – it was in the province of Minsk before the first war. Then it was in Poland. Now it is back in Russia again.'

Miss Granger handed the photograph back and Mrs Nowak sat with it in both hands as if it were a book and she had raised her eyes from it for a moment.

'That is how I learned Russian – they took us away. All the young men and women. Separately.'

'Took you away? Where to? Siberia?' Miss Granger intended this as a joke, then realized it was ill-timed.

But Mrs Nowak's expression did not change. Alight and charged, she lived in a passionate memory that did not include the prompter opposite.

'Oh yes. And it was so cold. I have never been so cold.

Everything froze. Your clothes' – she laid her hands on her breasts – 'were always damp. And the skin on your face' – she lifted her hands to knead her cheeks – 'went so terribly red and hard. We had only one stove in a long hut in the camp and we had to find the fuel. Oh, we burned everything. Once a week we would stand outside the huts all morning and wait for the trucks to come – and you know there you can see for miles and miles and all the same, and you would see them long before they reached you and wait for them to creep, creep across. They would have our food on there. All sorts of things. One week there would be sacks of turnips. Or oats. Or a sack of bread. Occasionally there would be dried fish. I don't know where they got that from out there. And sometimes they didn't come at all. But when the Germans invaded Russia – oh well, we were all friends then, I suppose, and they let us go and then we were in Baku and on a ship from Odessa and then in the British Army, you see, in Africa and Italy. And that's how it went.'

Mrs Nowak's chair creaked as she sat, musing, back; her blue gaze levelled on the other woman's face, her baggy skin aglow in the shadowed room.

Miss Granger fiddled with the photographs. She pointed at one.

'Did you know Stefan before the war?'

'Oh yes.' Mrs Nowak came doubly alive. 'And, Miss Granger, it was a miracle. Because I had known Stefan in the same town and we met again in the Army and that is where we married. In Italy. It was so funny because Stefan was only a corporal and I, I was a staff-sergeant – and I used to joke and say that I could order him to marry me if I wanted.' She started to laugh and her great slanting bosom rose and fell.

'You weren't engaged or anything – before the war?'

'No, no – we were not like that then, Miss Granger. You must know. Not like these silly English girls. Ugh.' She wrinkled her mouth. 'It makes me sick, really feeling sick. The office where I worked once – they would talk on and on all day about their boy-friends and sex, sex, sex – and what do you call it? ''Making love.'' What a horrible expression. Making love – what an expression. Like a machine. There is no romance. No. None. We all know what men and women have – we didn't take this ridiculous notice all the time. It is so childish, Miss Granger. No.'

She sorted through the photographs again.

'Now – here is Paris.' Mrs Nowak raised her knuckles to her mouth and blew a great gusting kiss across the table . . .

The lessons were virtually useless to her – as soon as the idea entered Miss Granger's head that what she was doing was slightly ridiculous, her interest began to die. For the next couple of weeks she had to force herself to concentrate on the study of grammar at home. But after a quarter of an hour or so she would lie down on her bed, her legs dangling over the side as if to remind herself that she could get up any time she chose – until she rolled into the middle of the bed and dozed, half-awake, for hours in an unhappy reverie. She blamed the heat of the summer, the new term drawing nearer, and she went down again to the Nowaks' house, which was cool and friendly.

This week they were on page fifty-seven and, afterwards, in Italy again. It was almost five before Miss Granger got away and then Mrs Nowak, seeing her out, said, 'Miss Granger, I almost forgot. Next week . . .'

Early on Monday morning, before dawn, she woke trembling from a dream.

From Mrs Nowak's memories of the Italian partisans, who, as Miss Granger sat listening, had finished their drinks and shouted out, 'We are going to hunt for Fascists.' They walked into the night and into her sleeping head in the comic gaiters and baggy pants of the *carabinieri*, wearing tricorn hats and pursuing in daylight Mouter through the catacombs of Highgate Cemetery, past Radclyffe Hall, around that huge, bird-dung-beshrounded mausoleum . . .

She woke trembling from the dream.

What was worse than this was lying awake in the dark.

She had to get up. Outside, lead turned to silver. In the chilly air of her kitchen she made a cup of coffee. She went back to bed. Sitting up, she pulled the clothes under her chin and felt at first cold, then warm again. At last she got out of bed and walked, dressing-gowned, to the living-room, and the sun came up somewhere behind the block and cast its humped shadow onto the yellow wall across the way, and miraculously, as she watched, all the dark lesions between the roofs, in the window frames, under the sills and the lintels of the doors were healed from deep shadow to a milky blue.

Today the new school year began.

Her bus ran down Junction Road, past the end of the street where the Nowaks lived. At nine, her flat was in a different country, a world ago.

She stared at her new class, at the virgin register. The early morning decayed in her memory, a series of diminishing echoes of the boom of the traffic, the voices of children coming in from the playground. After half an hour, though, the fog lifted from their faces. The white, pictured walls of the room and the orange bars of the desks defined the boy with the crooked glasses, the girl with corkscrew hair, the large-eyed, square-mouthed girl – Spanish. A brother higher up the school. They were most beautiful. They would remain most beautiful for a year as their teacher talked on and on of a mythical world which, unlike the real one, did not endlessly betray the young and old.

The bell rang, releasing them all.

She felt abnormally tired. On Wednesday, sitting alone in the staffroom in her free period, for no reason at all she began to cry. Mouter came in. 'Oh. I see. Sorry,' he said, and waved his hands without purpose in the air. He coughed, stalked too loudly across the room to the bookcase, hesitated, picked up a book. 'Ah.' He smiled nervously as he passed her and went out again.

On Friday she wrote to her brother. Perhaps, as he had said, he was thinking of leaving Zimbabwe soon. She hoped so. Things looked more hopeful there, she knew, but she would love to see him and little Michael again. *You have no roots there, after all* . . .

On Saturday afternoon she made her way down Junction Road again.

She turned into the street. Two-storey houses with steps going up to their doors. The front rooms bulged out over tiny areas and basement windows and gratings.

Number 17 was dingy, its windows sourly enlaced.

Number 19 had had the fancy stonework over the door (acorns and oak leaves round a sheaf of corn) picked out in yellow and purple paint.

Miss Granger went up the steps of Number 21. She rang the bell and waited, looking up the street.

Stefan opened the door. He seemed surprised to see her, but then he said, 'Yes, please come in, yes,' with an odd, impatient smile.

He led her into the back room; the window looked out to the garden wall, and the back windows of the next street, a bayonet of blue sky between their roofs.

'Miss Granger,' he announced.

Halina Nowak stood at the end of the dining-table. The plain white cloth had been taken off, and a richly embroidered scarlet and green cloth laid. A large, shallow bowl held a salad; a plate with slightly less than half a pork pie with a knot-ornamented crust; three slices of white, buttered bread; a bottle of what looked like red spirit, a quarter empty; a plate with a few grapes; another with one small saffron cake and crumbs — the remains of a feast for two.

'Miss Granger!' Mrs Nowak held a knife in one hand, a piece of pie in the other; her fat, dimpled, ochre arms filled and overflowed from the short sleeves of a white blouse. 'I thought we had said not this week.'

She remembered: *If you would mind, not next Saturday* . . .

'How stupid of me — of course you did. How ridiculous. I'm most awfully sorry.' Stefan was smiling as if in shared embarrassment at her side. 'It's your birthday, isn't it?'

'I am surprised. You forgetting?' said Mrs Nowak. 'Yes. My birthday. A sad occasion at my age. I'm not going to tell you how many years. Well. And it's such a fine day — the last we are going to have of the good weather, I think — that Stefan and I were going for a drive. Into the country.'

'Oh, do excuse me. I'll go.'

'No, no,' said Stefan.

'You must help us celebrate,' said Mrs Nowak. 'It's not such a big party, after all. Stefan.'

Stefan pulled out a chair from the table and beckoned, smiling, for her to sit down.

'You are a friend. And after so many weeks of that terrible language.' Mrs Nowak laughed. She hummed to herself as the knife hovered over the pie. 'You will have a piece? You look rather pale, my dear . . . I cannot keep calling you Miss Granger, can I? Not today.'

'Janice,' said Miss Granger.

'And fetch another glass, Stefan.'

'No, that is too much.'

But Mrs Nowak pushed the plate across the table.

I shan't stop, Miss Granger promised herself, I am a stranger – as Mrs Nowak bent again over the table, pouring drink into the glass that Stefan brought in.

'What is that? Whoa, whoa.'

Smiling, Mrs Nowak filled the glass to the brim.

'Vodka, of course. That I make myself.'

'You make the vodka yourself?' Miss Granger said incredulously.

'I'm sorry – that I mix myself, I should have said. It is mixed with the juice of cherries – real cherries, and we have all sorts in Poland, you know – pear and peach and, well, all sorts of fruit. It is pure spirit.'

Miss Granger did not often drink. She lifted the glass – one of those tall, waisted affairs in which saloon bars serve sherry – to her lips, and held her other hand cupped under to catch any drops. Over the glass, through the window, the garden wall was lit unreally by the sun. An upper sash window in the back of one of those houses in the next street had been pushed right up and a woman leaned over the sill, a look of suspicion on her face as she searched the invisible garden below.

She still wanted to leave – but Mrs Nowak had set herself on another interminable stream of reminiscence, of how the men had drunk in the war, in Poland, her father's plum vodka, the orchards, the long summer nights . . .

Stefan had retreated to the doorway, where he stood patiently, fingering a flat cap. How Polish he looks, how like a foreigner should look, how quintessentially . . . The liquor curled inside her.

'But you know – they were always gentlemen then, always,' Mrs Nowak was babbling to her. 'I remember . . .'

She had sipped the glass all the way down at last. Though Mrs Nowak pressed her to take another she said no, she really must be on her way, she mustn't keep them.

When she stood up she turned awkwardly out of her chair – Stefan now putting on his cap, pulling the back firmly down, smiling in that effortlessly kindly way – and one heel dug into the carpet and she stumbled. Stefan advanced smartly and held out his hands to steady her.

They will think I am drunk, she thought angrily. 'Oh,' she said. 'You must think I'm drunk.'

'Don't be silly,' said Mrs Nowak. 'My goodness, you're all right. You will not stay? You haven't eaten your pie.'

'No. I'll leave you to your drive. It will be a lovely day. It should be nice. It's such a nice day.'

Stefan stood away from the door to let her pass. Mrs Nowak followed her into the hall. 'We will see you next week then, let me . . .' but Miss Granger had turned the Yale knob herself and opened the front door.

She went down the steps feeling slightly tipsy, turned uncertainly at the bottom, and Mrs Nowak stood at the top and Stefan stood in the shadow of the hall and they waved, absurdly, as if she, not they, were going away somewhere.

The following Saturday she did not go for her lesson. She felt that she had intruded, offended somehow against the Nowaks' privacy. Another week passed. Her brother wrote back, angrily answering her letter, telling her not to pay any attention to the bloody Socialists in the English papers. Things were not getting better. He related – *God, I was bloody angry* – how the son of his houseboy Joseph, allowed to stay on a visit – *the last time that happens* – had told Michael that very soon, now that the Africans had taken over, the house and everything in it would belong to them – and James had told Joseph straight, had threatened to sack him for what the boy had said, but Joseph had pleaded to stay on and said he would not know what he would do if the Grangers ever left. *So, you see*, James wrote, *it's the young ones who want us to go. Joseph would be heartbroken. He has a job and £20 a month, which might not sound much but is a bloody good wage for a black* and more gossip and complaints about his own job, the family. *Love James. And Sarah*, his wife had written underneath.

'It's all over,' said Mouter. She had been talking to him about her brother. 'They can't see it. If I was him, I would get out while the going's still reasonably good. By the way, how's your old Polish girl – still ploughing on, are you?'

'She's very well.' Miss Granger looked suspiciously at Mouter. Was he laughing at her? No – licking his fingertip frequently, he was counting through a pile of duplicated sheets on the staffroom table. 'I haven't been for a couple of weeks.'

'Well, must press on, you know.' He went on counting the papers, dividing them into equal piles. 'Once you've started something.' Then he was silent. The big old library clock ticked the free period loudly away.

Mrs Nowak may have been well. Away from her – the large body seemed even larger and slightly comic in thinking about her. What was it, though, that these people had? Something she could never attain. A shared war? Love? No, more than that. A whole other country in their heads, precisely detailed and unaltering. The internal land that was at the same time regret and consolation for the exiled.

And what did she feel about the woman? A mixture of irritation and affection. The lessons had not been much use; they seemed to have grown shorter week by week as more and more time had been filched from them when a word or phrase would evoke another piece of Mrs Nowak's past.

Away for three weeks, in which time she had hardly looked at the notebook in which she had carefully printed – Russian handwriting being beyond her – new words, exercises, notes on grammar, now, when she looked back, the far-off, simple objects of the first lessons – bridge, tree, water, house, desk, husband, wife, Englishman and map – stood, sharply defined in their naked, disconnected holiday landscape, the paper characters speaking in absurdly inconsequential phrases their desires for chairs, sisters or the nearest pharmacy. And holes began to appear in the landscape where objects suddenly hid their meanings. What is that word? Oh, Life. *Zhin*. Known, but unpronounceable.

She would go down to Mrs Nowak's. She would not go down. Send a cheque for the unpaid lessons, with a letter expressing her regret that she could not continue? No, that would be intolerably rude after their kindnesses. Go down in the morning then, so there was no possibility of becoming ensnared in one of those afternoon sessions.

But again Mrs Nowak took matters out of her hands.

When Stefan opened the door he wore a worried look. He stared at her for a moment and then said, 'We haven't seen you for some time, Miss Granger.' He hesitated. 'But come in. I hope you haven't been ill.'

Mrs Nowak was in the back room. Stripping a pair of rubber gloves from her hands, she stood in the place she had occupied at the birthday party. But now her eyes were angry and unsettled. In the morning gloom her bulk, in the familiar brown dress, looked somehow less substantial.

Through the window, a little open at the top, from over the wall, out of the yard next door, rose a woman's voice in a chattering, indignant swarm of abusive words; then a man's voice soothing, but with an undertow of irritation. 'Now come on. Now come on in.'

But the high voice railed on. 'Bloody woman. I'll fix her. I'll fix you.' The voice stopped abruptly. 'I'll fix you,' came as a final, even more violent exclamation. A door slammed. Everything was quiet.

'Ooo-ooh,' half gasping, half moaning, Mrs Nowak shuddered. She raised her hands in a gesture of despair.

'Forgive me, Miss Granger, but these people next door . . . This has gone on for weeks now – and this, this morning for an hour now.'

Stefan shook his head.

'Oh yes. Oh yes,' Mrs Nowak insisted.

'It is at an end now,' said Stefan.

'There is no end,' said Mrs Nowak.

'They have gone. Sit down. And you too, please, Miss Granger. I will make some tea. Would you like a cup?'

'No, really. I can't stop.'

'You can drink tea,' said Mrs Nowak sharply, and subsided into her chair. Deflated, she sighed. Her face had lost its ruddy colour and was an unhealthy earth-yellow.

Miss Granger sat down slowly and reluctantly. 'What on earth is the matter?' she asked.

'These people. They are ruining the street – those and those like them. Soon we will have nothing, believe me.' She sagged back in her chair and waved a hand vaguely at the window; then she began again, in a slow, measured way, trying to keep her anger down. 'That – that woman next door. Her child is walking on the top of the wall this morning and I ask him – quite polite – to get down. Would he? Oh no; without a word he goes on walking, looking straight in front. And I say to him again to get down – or – or I shall call his mother. Then I hear her. On the other side of the wall. And she is not telling the boy to get off, but shouting. And such vile language – and Stefan is trying to sleep, you know, this morning because now he is on late shift at the factory on Friday night. It is impossible. This is only the latest row between next door. Impossible. It was so quiet when we came here . . .' She stopped and stared across at Miss Granger. 'I'm sorry – it is none of your problems. But,' she looked down at her watch, 'you are early. And where have you been?'

'Yes. You see, I can't come. Not . . .'

Stefan came into the room with the tea-tray.

'. . . not this afternoon, and I remembered . . .'

The racket started again in next door's yard: the woman's shrill voice resuming where it had left off; the man's voice again mediating, but angrier now.

'It is impossible,' cried Mrs Nowak. 'You see how they are.'

Stefan said, 'I will go. I will go,' and went out.

But by the time Mrs Nowak, half raised on her elbow in the chair and staring intensely through the window, saw him appear in the garden, the neighbours had shut up and gone again.

Perhaps, thought Miss Granger, they are like the figures I saw on that clock in Bavaria, who come out every hour, turn, pirouette, bow, curtsy, raise musical instruments, hammers or hats. Then there is a great whirring, and the hour begins to dribble out. A tiny preparatory pre-echo of a chime and the blacksmith's hammer comes down, and boom the hour bell goes, the clock whirrs again, the hammer is raised, the hats are put on, the trombones and clarinets are lowered from scarlet lips, click, click, and off they roll, stiffened, the door clapping shut behind them.

Stefan stood listening under the wall. The two women watched him. He turned away, and disappeared from view coming back into the house.

'You see how it is – since they came?' Relaxing, Mrs Nowak slumped down in her chair. 'They are ruining the country – these blacks all over.'

Oh God, it is my brother all over again, thought Miss Granger. Out of this mouth.

'You cannot call this country yours, Miss Granger. How can you? It is a mongrel nation – and they are breeding so fast and have so many children. It is terrible. This street was so quiet and pleasant when we came. But now!'

'Come now, Mrs Nowak. One family – it's hardly fair, is it? That you should, well, all these . . . these people, well, because you have unpleasant neighbours.'

'One family? Wait, my dear, wait until your classrooms are full of little black faces, or not so little – all staring and hating.'

'That is a horrible thing to say, Mrs Nowak. That is an appalling thing. You should know better.'

'Eh?' Mrs Nowak smiled pityingly. 'I do know better. The English are all the same. Your race is all mixed blood of Jews and Irish and now these.'

'I must go. I must. I cannot stand any longer hearing you. That is silly and wicked and untrue.'

'True,' said Mrs Nowak, with a terrible complacency.

Miss Granger scrabbled her handbag and gloves and newspaper together off the table. 'You should remember, Mrs Nowak, that you are a guest of this country and have come – ' but she couldn't go on. She was at once in a rage near hysteria, which swept involuntarily through her body and closed her throat, though her mouth was open, and her arms waved agitatedly in the air. Mrs Nowak sat back in her chair, bubbling with laughter at the sight of her.

'I can't stand it any more. To hear you talk,' Miss Granger gabbled, and she turned her back and stalked from the room. At first she went the wrong way down the hall, into a lobby, shadowy and musty, of coats, long and short, bulging from both walls. Swivelling round, she passed the doorway of that room again, did not look in, but let herself be ridden to the front door with the 'How silly, Miss Granger – like a child,' that Mrs Nowak called from the room, that rang in her ears as she opened the door, went down the steps, the street.

To learn a language is to be a child again. But then the world is expanding, not contracting. Now there were only the simplest words left in Miss Granger's head, like the drawings pinned to the walls in an infants' school: I, chair, table, house, I.

She sent a cheque, without a letter, to pay for the lessons.

For the rest of that autumn, and in the winter, spring and summer terms Miss Granger rode on the top deck of the bus to school. Sometimes the traffic locked at the mouth of the street where the Nowaks lived. Looking out sometimes, she would see Stefan's old white Zephyr parked, one side hanging down to the kerb.

She was reading when the bus passed and did not see there was an ambulance outside the house, and neither, a month later, did she see the two black cars.

In winter the buses went on strike for a day and Miss Granger was forced to walk. She chose the side of Junction Road away from the stinking chain of cars bound for the city. A little snow lay on the roofs – and on the Heath, where this morning she had seen a red-sweatered dash of a man standing still while his brown dot of a dog ran mad for joy in the stiff white grass.

Coming along, she raised her look from the pavement to avoid someone hurrying past. Stefan Nowak turned the next corner, a small, busy, capped figure in a fawn overcoat with an imitation fur collar.

Miss Granger's heart gave a bump as she saw him. She almost stopped. She wondered whether to speak, but as they drew near she gave only a silly, embarrassed smile. Stefan saw a woman approaching whose step suddenly faltered and who gave him an odd, crooked smile. But she did not stop and he did not recognize her, though he thought he should.

The pavement was slippery with black ice.

'Pardon,' he said, smiling too, tipped his cap, and side-stepped to avoid her as they passed.

Are You Coming to Jerusalem?

Patrick saw the man who lived in the park come out of the park. Even from up here, by the traffic-lights at the junction of the road that sloped down to the park, there was no mistaking him. The man was very tall and thin and his long staff seemed to pole him upwards in great strides.

Patrick retreated from the lights. He knew every one of the shops on both sides of the wide road and they all knew the boy. And his red-faced father. The early Saturday-morning shoppers absorbed him in their contrary rivers. He got up to the off-licence. They didn't open until ten; he stood in front of the metal shutter. Over the road, Jimmy Crane, who went drinking with Patrick's dad, wiped beads of rain off the motorbikes' long saddles. Bodiless leathers and black-visored helmets hung in the window of the lean-to that was his shop.

Patrick looked down to the lights. Suddenly, the man was on the wide pavement, knapsack bouncing rhythmically on one high, bony shoulder-blade, his cropped grey head nodding fiercely among the shoppers. His clothes seemed too small, his wrists protruded from a green canvas jacket, his brown trousers rode inches above his boots.

The man stopped one door down from Patrick. Outside the Health Food Store. His mouth opened.

'Where wast thou' — the words were bellowed in a high, urgent tone — 'when I laid the foundations of the earth?' He struck the pavement with his staff. 'Declare, if thou hast understanding.' He twisted his head on his long neck as if in pain. A woman hurried past him, crowding her shopping-bags protectively round her knees. Patrick thought the man was drunk. He expected a joke next. His father when drunk sometimes sang a song about someone called McCaffery and after stopping, with tears in his eyes, told a joke if there was company. But there was no joke. Just the stone-coloured head moving from side to side, then stopping, to shout.

'Whereupon are the foundations thereof fastened? Who laid the corner stone thereof?'

The walking staff that seemed half as long as the street waved at the shop windows. Then he was off again. Off, past the shops, the block of flats, the gabled houses, that high-stepping mechanical-looking gait carrying him swiftly away.

Jimmy Crane was standing over Patrick. 'You all right?' he asked. 'I've been shouting at him to bugger off.'

'Why?'

Jimmy didn't answer directly. 'Couldn't get across sooner. Bloody traffic.' He frowned after the dwindling man and flexed his broad shoulders irritably, like a boxer warming up.

'Who is he?' asked Patrick.

'Riff-raff. Rubbish. Don't bother. Always preaching or

bawling about something. Taken to coming round here. You steer clear of him.'

'Does he live in the park?'

'Eh?' Jimmy looked puzzled for a moment. 'Shouldn't be surprised. He's not all there.' His hand, which had slid loosely onto Patrick's shoulder, gripped tightly.

'Ow. That hurts.'

Jimmy laughed. 'It doesn't, does it?' he said, and pressed again.

Patrick tried to imagine the preacher living in the park but found it hard. Although you could see the park – a huge tract of common land with pine-trees on bare rises and holly woods in deeps and a lake glimpsed through trees – the lights were the official limit of Patrick's world. His dad said he mustn't go down on his own; on the other side of the park the houses were slummier, the people rougher; over there they had shut a hospital somewhere and let the poor bloody nutters out to fend for themselves.

Patrick saw two more who appeared on the street after crossing the park: a fat old woman with bulging black plastic bin-bags strung about her body so that she looked as if she had been pumped grotesquely up and then lashed round with string; and a thin young man with brown hair standing stiffly up from his forehead, whose mild spasticity propelled him lurching forward, his arms and legs appearing to clutch at the air. But these appeared and passed away, not to return. The preacher came round at least once a week, furiously striding the pavement. He came always from the direction of the park. Until one Saturday evening in the early summer.

His dad was saying something about Patrick not understanding. 'You'll understand when you're older. Sometimes I have to be on me own or with a bit of company.' The great red-pocked face turned away. The hands fumbled in the trouser pockets. 'Pat – here's a couple of quid. Get yourself some sweets. Or something. You can come up again when you see the curtains are open.'

He led the boy to the door and watched him down the iron-railed steps, then heard him go, trainers flapping, the next three flights down to the street door. Then he went back into the small flat and drew the curtains.

It was summer, warm, and would be light until late on. The street had been picked up and its upper windows dipped in gold. Patrick tried to look as if he were on an errand. To the off-licence; for fags for his dad. He would hurry up there, go past, return slowly, buy some sweets. Then sit in the bus-shelter over the road and eat them. Make the future up from there. The future in minutes. Go back outside the flat, knowing that his dad would be nowhere near through.

He went to the off-licence. He crossed the road. Jimmy Crane was just coming out, locking up the motorbike shop. 'Where you off to then, Pat?' His hand twisted the boy's upper arm with a jovial roughness. His hand reeked of the stuff he used to get the oil off; the rest of him of after-shave lotion. His beer-belly fell forward in a brilliantly white shirt.

'Getting Dad some fags,' Patrick lied.

'Walk down with me. You can have a pop from the boozer.' They walked on. 'Dad locked you out again, has he?' For some reason Jimmy chuckled. When they got to the pub on the corner he told Patrick to wait outside the bar door. After a couple of minutes he came out with a Coke and a big bag of crisps. 'I'll be a while,' he said. 'But then I'll take you back home. We'll get the dirty what's-it out.' He went back in, laughing.

Patrick sat in the brick alcove of the bus-shelter. Above him was a frame for the time-tables. It was empty, the glass long gone, the plywood back-board signed 'L loves S' in black felt. The sun was lowering itself over the park. A tall lamp-post and the telephone box cast shadows in front of the alcove; one long, thin and capped, the other stumpy, panelled with dusty light.

At last he placed the empty bottle under the bench and kicked it back with his heel. It rolled out again. He got up and wandered to the traffic-lights. They were green but he only had to wait for one ambling car before crossing. From this side of the road he could see the heads above the frosted-glass bottom half of the bar window. He couldn't see Jimmy. The heads opened their mouths and spoke and laughed and yawned and called, all in silence. They raised mugs and glasses to their lips, puffed and sucked at cigarettes. A man in shirt-sleeves came, his face beaming, out of the door and out with him came a murmuring, rising and falling roar, a woman's whooping laugh.

Patrick looked down to the park gates. A man with a dog was going in. He looked the other way.

And here, coming along fast, was the tall man. There was nothing between him and Patrick. Every moment he drew nearer and taller, the pale eyes searching above Patrick for the far pine-trees on their knolls.

Patrick expected him to sweep on by and cross the junction. But the man halted a yard away.

'I walked with the Lord,' he shouted in that great cracked voice. His head turned restlessly. 'Do you know where Jerusalem is?' he demanded of the empty pavement, the closed shops. 'The Lord of Hosts said – if thou will walk in my ways, and if thou shall keep my charge and my courts, I will give thee places to walk among these that stand now.'

The preacher's terrible pale stare turned down on Patrick. 'And the streets of the city shall be full of boys and girls playing.

Why aren't you playing, boy? Because this is not Jerusalem. You
know that? This is nowhere near to Jerusalem. Here, take it. Take
it.' The tall man thrust out a fat black book. 'This is your map and
staff. Are you coming to Jerusalem? Are you?'

Close to, he had small, yellow, irregular teeth. His face was a
folded grey sack with a mouth cut in. He was stuffing the book
back in his haversack. 'Are you coming?' he whispered, and his
long bony hand shot stiffly out and gripped Patrick's wrist.

Then it was as if they were flying, walking all at once at a
tremendous pace towards the forbidden park. They were through
the gate. They swept into a gravelled track overhung by huge
oaks, a red pole across the mouth to keep out cars. Halfway
down, the man stopped. He let go Patrick's wrist. 'You must get
off the road. All off the road,' he shouted, and loped away
between the trees.

The preacher stood in a clearing, tall among lowered branches.
The chin had sunk almost to his chest, the lips moved; a
dreaming, whispering statue. 'Are you there? Are you there? That
place I want. It's not there any more. Nothing there.' The pale
eyes stared, miles past Patrick. 'I've been looking for it. That's
what I'm looking for.' His voice was not the hectoring, mad voice
of the street, but low and urgent, entreating a favour. 'They are
making wars and pains and moving the streets so I cannot find it.
We are not the only people in the world. There are angels. Devils
watch from the windows. They whisper in the tap. Something has
happened.' He took a step forward.

Patrick swung round, catching his jumper on a twig. Tearing
free, he ran at full pelt up the avenue, past the pole. Head down,
he did not dare to think how far away the gate was, how much
further the safety of the shops. In terror, he collided with the
hard-soft trunk of a man. Arms circled him; in his struggle to get
free he seemed to drown in the man.

'Steady on, Pat. Steady on. It's me – Jimmy.'

The voice came through the drowning water and faded up into the evening. Jimmy held him longer than Patrick wanted. He pulled away, panting, and looked over his shoulder. The avenue was clear.

'You all right? He didn't do anything to you?'

Patrick shook his head.

'Because if he did, by God . . .' Jimmy blustered.

The preacher appeared in the avenue, his elongated shadow reaching almost to them.

'Wait here,' Jimmy commanded. 'I'll see him off. Eh. Eh, you,' he shouted.

But ignoring, not even registering the man and the boy, the preacher hitched up his pack and strode away up the avenue, his shadow following, swaying like a dancer.

'He didn't do anything,' Patrick insisted.

'No, no.' His father was breathing hard. Suddenly he covered his eyes with one great hand. Patrick was afraid of what was concealed under that hand. Nothing. His father drew it slowly down, massaging his red cheeks.

'Whatever . . . I don't know . . .' He looked at his hand, at the boy. 'Go to bed now, Pat,' he said. 'I shan't go out tonight.'

Patrick got up from the chair at the kitchen table. His father stared after him as the boy went to the door.

'I'll have to keep you in,' he said. 'I will. You should be looked after better.'

Patrick went into the small bedroom. He didn't put on the light. His bed was under the window; his father's pushed against the opposite wall. He heard his father turning over knives and spoons in the kitchen drawer, opening and shutting a cupboard;

he heard him curse softly. Then he heard him go into the living-room and the soft plop of a can being opened.

Patrick knelt on his bed. He looked down at the orange crossing-beacons flashing off and on. Above the roofs no stars could be seen. Further down, a woman came out of the off-licence. She held a white tissue-wrapped bottle and hurried away, holding the bottle tightly in against her breast. He wondered where the shouting man was. When he would appear again at this point on his orbit, shouting to the golden street. What it must be like to live under the silent, dark trees.

The Elements

When Stuart first joined the company he had been introduced to everyone in all the other offices. Then he was shown his desk. The desk opposite, he was told, was Henry Paisley's. But Henry wasn't in today. Nor the next, but on Wednesday – Stuart having taken a few orders over the phone and beginning to like the feel of the big, half-empty office – Henry came in.

His clothes were ill-fitting. They were like the clothes Stuart's father wore when gardening. A dark-grey, green-striped jacket from a suit; a pair of brown corduroy trousers, pale and balding at the knees; a tartan tie – 'The Paisley,' said Henry proudly, smoothing it down over his huge, shelving belly. The tie was not clean.

Henry went to the pub every lunch-time and came back late. He would sometimes disappear in mid-afternoon also and reappear, half an hour later, standing at the desk, looking as if he did not quite recognize it. That first day he invited Stuart to join him at lunch.

They came out of the side entrance of the Cold Storage Company and walked a little way, right, left, into the back of Smithfield, just behind St Bartholomew's. The pub was on a corner, with the door propped open to the warm June day. 'A pint?' asked Henry. 'Two bitters, please. Pints. Two Scotch eggs. Cheese sandwich.' Another pint – Stuart lingered over his second while Henry sank a third. When they returned to the office Stuart felt like going to sleep. He missed his footing in the corridor in front of the Sales Manager and grazed the wall with his shoulder.

'Take more water with it,' said the Sales Manager.

Stuart was nineteen, nearly twenty, and this was only his second job. The first had been in an insurance company. He felt he could do better. He had A-levels in Biology and Geography ('Very apt,' said Henry) and wanted to put them to some use before he forgot them. Now he worked for one of the largest meat importers in London. They had their own refrigerated ships that went to and from Argentina – a coloured aerial photograph of one hung on the wall behind the Sales Manager's desk.

On the first Friday, Henry gave him the week's orders to total. A roll of cool grey figures curled from the adding machine on his desk. In the corner behind him, a small television monitor – its screen silent, grey, particularly dead – peered from its corrugated paper wrapping; the first visual display unit of the new computer system. 'When's it coming on stream?' someone asked Henry. 'Buggered if I know,' said Henry, and Stuart watched as they stood discussing it for a few minutes. At lunch, Henry took him to the pub again.

Stuart was surprised to see all the office managers there, with some of the outside salesmen. A director was buying. Everyone seemed to ask for halves. Stuart asked for a half. Henry had a pint and stood, massive and gloomy, on the edge of the crowd. He took a tin cigarette-rolling machine from his pocket and began to pack big woolly strands of tobacco between the rollers. 'Bloody hell,' said the director, 'give him a proper fag, someone, for Christ's sake.' Everyone laughed and the smokers hurried to produce cigarettes. The winner leaned over and offered his packet with a patronizing smile. Henry blushed, jammed the machine rollers together with one hand and accepted a cigarette with the other.

'How goes it?' said one of the salesmen to Stuart. He listened very attentively and seemed most interested in all Stuart had to say.

Stuart was happy.

He liked the idea of himself. He was tall and his body was well proportioned, thanks to his family's careful heredity and to the games he had played enthusiastically at his school. Intelligent – within reason – personable, he was attractive to the sort of girls to whom he was attracted; the latest of these being Sonia Michaels. She was the one. She had been for the past six months. He gave her flowers and records. Over and over in his bedroom he played the same love-songs that he had bought for her. He sang under his breath in the office. She was the first girl he had ever properly made love to. That was on a Sunday afternoon at her parents' house. Her father had gone to the golf club; her mother to church. For some reason Stuart and Sonia found themselves together in the hallway. Sonia, leaning against the frame of the door to the kitchen, smiled up at him as he went to pass. Her face was flushed. Behind him, bright sunlight spilled through the coloured glass sunbeams in the front door; red, orange, lilac, purple. They kissed. Without a word he followed her upstairs.

He stood in her room. 'Is this it?' he said, in what was meant to be a jokey tone; but his voice sounded hoarse and far-off. There were bunk beds for her and her sister; a view of suburban, hedged gardens out of the window. A stuffed Snoopy leaned against one wall, a framed Guide's certificate above his muzzle. Bottles and cosmetics on the stripped-pine dressing-table – its slightly tilted mirror reflected from her back to the carpet. They kissed again and suddenly began to undo their jeans as quickly as they could. They hurried each other into the lower bunk bed. He fumbled and she guided him. Worried, he could not tell if she were a virgin or not. In a few moments, during which he felt surprisingly little, he apologized for coming so quickly. 'It won't always be like that,' he assured her.

That was three months ago; they were to be married next week.

Stuart was to have a proper stag night – one with his real friends, almost all of them the children of his father's friends. The party was to be held at the local pub on the side of the golf-course at Muswell Hill. But office custom and precedent demanded that he take his colleagues out for a drink at least. With bravado masking his fear of a refusal, Stuart invited the Sales Manager. 'You too, Mr Wood,' he said to the director, who lolled back in the chair under the window.

'Good of you. When is it?'

'Thursday night. Next Thursday night.'

'Thursday? Odd night. Why Thursday?'

'Day off Friday,' said the Sales Manager. 'Recover his strength for Saturday.'

'Oh yes.' The director gave a dirty laugh and glanced up at Stuart. Then he began to study the papers on his lap. The manager indicated with a nod of his head that the interview was at an end.

'Congratulations,' said Henry rather heavily, after lunch. He leaned on the desk, splaying his short, thick fingers on the blotter. The fingers seemed to have no nails at all. 'You are going to have a drink with us?' he asked. Surprisingly, he sounded almost anxious.

'Yes, I thought . . .'

'Good.' Henry had appointed himself organizer of the company booze-up. He swept away, mumbling, 'I'll go and see Geoff,' before Stuart could say anything else.

'We'll start off at the Blackfriars,' said Henry when he returned, 'then see how we go.'

At a quarter to five on Thursday afternoon Henry, looking worried, came up to him in the corridor.

'Can you make your own way down to the pub?' he asked. 'I've got to meet a friend of mine at five. I'll bring him down. Don't mind, do you? He's from the North and staying a few days with us. All right if I bring him along? OK? See you down there.'

A little party gathered in the office at five to accompany Stuart. There were two clerks from Import; a Newcastle lad from the cold store; a man Stuart had never seen before; and three of the girls from Accounts. A poor turn-out; no sign of the Sales Manager or director, and Stuart blamed Henry.

In the pub the men pressed him to the bar, the three girls chattered and stirred behind them, then scampered across to get seats at a table. Stuart passed drinks back to be relayed to the table. All afternoon he had been afraid that some embarrassing ritual would have to be gone through before he would be allowed to leave the premises. He remembered the sight once of one of the girls at the factory where his father worked in the offices. As Stuart had come walking up the street everyone was leaving for the night. The girl had emerged suddenly from the front doors.

She was wearing a top hat covered in sequins and trailing ribbons. Long skeins of pink and blue toilet paper were pinned to her blouse and, somehow attached to her skirt, hugely inflated condoms floated and bounced and bobbed about her as she ran, head down between the other girls. They pelted her with rice and confetti made from paper punches and telex tapes. The tiny white dots speckled her as she stumbled up the street, falling away to the pavement as the girls followed, yelping with laughter. Thank God they only did that to women.

The large bar was full at half-past five. People stood two or three deep at the bar; the men with their shirts pulled to one side, their collars open. It was a warm evening; the faces that came in glistened briefly in the outside glare, glowed red in the curtained bar.

Henry came in. His friend was tall, thin and very pale. His eyes floated behind thick spectacles. He carried a travelling bag and a pigskin briefcase. He went straight to the bar. Henry came over to the table.

'I thought, after this, we'd go up the road,' he said.

But, really, it was quite good after all. The drink seemed to sink in, eddy down, then flourish up in deepened voices, flushed faces, the beautiful green eyes and soft lips of Sandra, one of the Accounts girls, he found encircled by his arm. People laughed at his jokes; he laughed at theirs. And, laughing, some of them disappeared. Sandra disappeared; the other girls from Accounts were not there when he looked round. The men drew closer, impersonating a crowd.

Then they were on the street and heading for the next pub. They went up towards Ludgate Circus, five men, arm in arm, singing *The Blaydon Races* in strongly affected Geordie accents. They swung across the street, high-kneed and foreshortened in a tall, angled, dark mirror deep in a shop window. *Oh, me boys, yuh should a seen us gangin'. . .*

'I tell you,' said Henry's friend, leaning across the table. In his hand was a ball of gin and tonic that had been topped up twice already with large gins. 'This is the first decent pub I've been in tonight. Isn't it?' he said, turning belligerently to Henry, who was getting up to go to the bar again. 'You're getting married, aren't you?' he asked Stuart. He belched softly. 'Pardon,' he said.

Now there were only the three of them left. They were somewhere else. It was darker and smaller. What had been the summer evening now settled around and hugged them. Stuart was smoking a cigarette. He never smoked. Soon after, he begged another.

They stand by a bus-stop. The night cartwheels overhead; blue-black at ten o'clock. They are walking along a road. A sharp smell of urinous, green-yellow privet – though now the leaves are blue; a fine scent of wallflowers and the heavy odour of green-black laurel; the stars wobble and glint around dark patches of sky like the ends of broken bottles. Here is a gate. A path. Two steps. A door. The hallway is lit with one unshaded bulb. They are sitting in a room. Stuart is alone on a sofa. Now a woman is sitting by him. She is very attractive but quite old – oh, thirty at least. She is lighting a cigarette. She smiles at him. She tosses her long, straight, brown hair back and smoke spumes from her pursed lips.

The room is small, made smaller, compacted down on him by the weight, the oppression of hundreds of books – on shelves, in cabinets – and by, above and between the books, pictures of all sizes: Rowlandson, Ernst, Balthus, Etty, Caspar Friedrich; photographs of Mae West, Bertrand Russell, Charlie Parker, Karl and Groucho Marx – Stuart recognizes none of them except the

Marxes. All are old. On the door is pinned, blown up to grey, grainy life-size, a photograph of the woman sitting beside him. In the picture she is standing nude in this room.

She was drawing on her cigarette and listening to Henry. He waved his hands about, pointing out objects he thought would be of interest to Stuart. There was too much. Apart from the books and odd pictures there were shelves and drawers holding porcelain, stamps, coins, little bronzes, postcards, cigarette-cards and curios of all sorts. The centre of the small room was taken by a large plant growing from a green glass carboy. In one corner was a large fishtank a quarter filled with seaside pebbles – on them, curled, sleeping, was a snake.

The top of the head of Henry's friend could be seen over the end of the sofa. Stuart shifted and looked down at him. The man was lying on a sack chair – one of those bags filled with plastic beads – and he rolled himself gently from side to side and arched himself up and down to get comfortable. He saw Stuart and struggled to raise himself. 'Odd, isn't it,' he said, 'the elements we are composed of – calcium, carbon, phosphorus, sodium and all – if we burn we give off the same spectra as the stars.' He got up, banged against a bookcase and then, inevitably, walked into a small, delicate table as he tried to avoid it. He rode back with the door, slid along the wall and out. A hand reappeared to pull the door to. The woman, now established as Henry's wife, followed the friend. The door closed.

Henry was asking him something and holding out a bottle.

Music ran non-stop. Now it was blues. To Stuart it sounded like the Rolling Stones, but the picture of an old black man on the sleeve made him feel contemptuous. This was old, middle-aged

people's party stuff, drunk's stuff. The voice sang of love and
pity.

'How . . .' Stuart started to say, and the word came out as a
strangulated howl. He tried again. 'How'll do you think we'll,
well, do this year, er, ner, Henry?'

'Eh?' Henry was rapt, listening to the music.

'Er, how – in the office situation – do you think I'm doing?'

'Oh fine. Fine. Did you know I was leaving?'

'Ner. No. Sorry to hear . . .'

The next record clacked down and noise, half-shouting, half-
crying, came from some instrument he couldn't recognize.

'Ornette Coleman,' said Henry. 'This is a fabulous bit in a
minute. Listen.' And Henry turned a control on the old-
fashioned stereo and the terrible noise filled the room.

'They gave me the sack,' Henry shouted over the music. 'The
sack.'

It was a remarkable house. All up the walls, as Stuart climbed the
narrow staircase, were more pictures and posters; at the top a
home-made collage made from cut-up magazines and mounted,
peeling, on plasterboard, showed at its centre the nose of a B52
bomber entering a huge, half-opened scarlet-lipsticked pair of
lips. On the landing he pushed past a revolving bookcase; the
passage to the bathroom was lined shoulder-high on both sides
with yet more books. Only in the bathroom was there remission.
On an otherwise empty clothes-horse a pair of tights hung into
the bath. Stuart stood, swaying, over the lavatory bowl; cracks in
the lino all around ran out like cords in a spider's web.

When he got down again, the main light in the living-room had
been turned off. Henry's bulk partly obscured the red-shaded
lamp in the corner. With a scalpel he was cutting into a small
piece of something that looked like hard chocolate slightly furred

with green mould. Cut, it showed a shiny surface like soft stone. Henry crumbled the cut piece onto a book on his lap. In front of him on the table were his cigarette machine, a box of papers, a tin of tobacco, the stub of a candle in a saucer, and a dirty spoon.

He lit the candle. Placing flakes of the brown stuff in the spoon he held it over the flame. Stuart watched as they melted to a bubbling, oily tar from which wisps of acidly sweet smoke rose. Henry took the spoon from the flame. He had a paper ready filled in the rollers of his machine and he began to smear some of the sticky resin with a matchstick across the shreds of tobacco.

Now the music sounded as if it had been stretched. Henry's wife came back into the room. Henry's friend tiptoed in after her and resumed his place on the sack chair. Henry made another thin joint and passed it to his friend. He sucked at it, then smoke escaped weakly from his mouth and nostils. His face relaxed, but still did not lose its expression of profound misery.

'What happened in the kitchen?' Henry asked his wife.

'Oh, stupid Bernard knocked a couple of plates off the sink.'

Stuart had heard nothing – it must have happened while he was upstairs.

Bernard passed the joint back without saying anything. He raised a tumbler, nearly full of gin, to his lips. Then he lit an ordinary cigarette and sipped and inhaled alternately. When he stopped doing either he looked as if he were dead.

Henry took down a black plastic photograph album. He passed it over to Stuart. 'I think you'll find these quite interesting,' he said. Henry lay back in the big swivel armchair.

Stuart took a moment to realize just what the pictures on the first page showed. His face grew hot and he glanced up, blushing.

Henry's wife looked down at him, her eyelids half-closed, with some sort of contempt. Henry smiled.

In their harshly chemical oranges and pinks and reds the photographs illustrated Stuart's dreams, and the dreams he would have now. There were women with enormous breasts sitting on men; girls with breasts no bigger than halved pears, their legs apart, displaying – their fingers acting as surgical clamps – such openings to such coral-pink vaginas – for as long as he looked. He turned the page, wanting to linger, but not wanting to be seen doing so. Now men with enormous erect penises crammed them into every orifice of endlessly compliant partners. A page of black and white pictures in which a group of plain girls in school uniforms gathered in a cheaply furnished room around a naked man who lay on the floor masturbating. Stuart turned over. Two dark-haired, large-eyed homosexuals held each other's identical staff – as if in some trick mirror one reached through to touch his image.

Henry chuckled. 'Incredible, some of them, aren't they?' he said. 'But at least they look as if they're enjoying themselves. Go on, though. Look at the rest. They get better.'

The music was a slurping, breathy tenor saxophone. 'Ben Webster,' said Bernard, from the floor. Henry's wife was asleep in the chair. Henry was standing, waiting for the record to finish. The second bottle of whisky was three-quarters empty.

Stuart sat with the closed album on his lap. There were many pictures he wanted to look at again. But the intense excitement he had felt, the drink, the frustration, the fluctuation of blood between his legs, had exhausted him. He looked at his watch in the dim red light. It was quarter to five. His feet were swollen in his shoes, his mouth foul.

He got up to go to the lavatory again. Henry nodded at him and went on putting records in their sleeves.

Washing his hands, Stuart raised his face to the mirror. For one moment he did not recognize the person who stared out at him. The face was older; behind the slim nose was the fattened ghost of his father's nose. The cheeks were grey, the eyes tired out. He stood back, and smoothed his suit with his hands. He did not know where his tie had gone. And suddenly he felt that he would have to go now without seeing these people again – Henry, Henry's wife, the friend. Standing in their bathroom, he knew already they were far away, in the past – to be escaped from.

He eased himself down the stairs, pressing his hands against the few bare patches of wall to try and lighten his step on the creaking stairs. In the tiny hallway he listened. Behind the door the music droned on. He heard Henry cough. Then he took hold of the Yale lock and let himself out, holding the tongue of the lock back with his fingers until the door was nearly closed, he shut it with only a gentle click.

The morning was cold, a pale blue light already among the roofs.

He walked a couple of back streets, not knowing where he was until he came out on Brixton Hill. He caught the first bus of the morning, or the last bus of the night. As he sat alone on the upper deck, the pictures came up in front of him.

There were just the sexual organs, set in bodies that were only glimpsed as a sort of surround. There were no faces. He wished he had asked for one of the pictures. One he could keep and . . .

He started. The conductress was at his side, a tired-looking black woman who glared coldly down at him. She went away. The pictures clarified again immediately. If he could remember, hold on – to that position, bend her body into that receptive posture, cause her to be suspended above him, perfect, technicolour, odourless; Sonia.

Then he was ashamed. But he simply couldn't keep her out of their company. She joined avidly in all the orgies in his head.

He tried to think of something else. He searched the high blank wall of the Oval for Sonia's face, saw it for a moment, then his mind insisted on her legs, her breasts, and they in turn were lost, imposed upon and dissolved in the truncated limbs and sexual tackle of those better-remembered lovers under the photographer's brilliant light.

He ran his tongue over his uncleaned teeth.

How, he wondered about Henry and Henry's wife and his friend, how could they bear to live like that?

The Thames stretched dull and blond on either side as his bus swung onto Vauxhall Bridge.

Even in Dreams, He Thought, We Lie

He never knew how his father died. He only knew, because she moved in straight after the letter came, that Aunt V must have had something to do with it. For some time after his mother would say, 'Your dad would have liked this,' or, 'When Bob was here . . .' But she stopped speaking like that in front of Aunt V, and soon his father dwindled back into the photograph-frame on the dining-room sideboard.

The two women sat every night in the dining-room and Aunt V talked about the neighbours: about the women who were tarts, the men who were idle, and the children who were noisy and dirty and whose rushing about had nearly knocked her over this morning and yesterday morning and would tomorrow morning unless a constable intervened and weren't there laws about footballs in the street and bicycles on the pavement, as much as anyone cared nowadays?

His mother said only, 'Oh, I'm sure they mean no harm . . .'

Colin was forbidden to play in the street.

His white face appeared at the front bedroom window for half an hour at a stretch. Up the street he could hear the children shouting.

In 1950, he marched lead soldiers across his crumpled bed. The soldiers were Guards in charge of the Empire, with short red coats and tall black busbies whose paint came off in tiny specks on his fingers. The soldiers were hollow, so that great rents could be made in their chests with the pointed steel shells that the little spring-loaded field gun fired. Sometimes he would get up and go round the bed to be the enemy commander. From there the hills were differently shaped; the soldiers lurched forward to the gun.

Evening faded the battles. Then, to terrify himself, he would stand at the window and look up as the vast, starred sky replaced the blue dome above the houses.

The area they lived in was not good. 'Practically a slum,' said Aunt V. She persuaded his mother that the local primary school was not at all suitable for Colin. So he was taken out of there and dressed in a green and white striped cap, a green blazer with white-piped edges, grey shorts, grey socks and black shoes.

This was the uniform of his new school, a mile away, on the edge of the suburbs. The school was run by a genuine BA from Oxford. Mr Cassell. Not *Castle*, he insisted, but Cas-sell. A board in the overgrown front garden announced The Bevis Preparatory School For Boys. A short gravel path led to the black wooden porch of a large red Victorian house. It had been a rectory; the church next door had been bombed and never rebuilt. 'So, you see, we have no chapel facilities as such at the moment . . .' Mr Cassell explained to Aunt V at the interview.

Fortunately the school let out its pupils a quarter of an hour earlier than the state primary, so, by running all the way, Colin was able most times to avoid the jeers of the local children.

At home, his mother calling hello from the kitchen, he went upstairs to put away his things.

He had to pass Aunt V's room.

Sometimes, if she had just come in, the door would be open. The curtains were always half-drawn on the sash window; two hats, like bowlers, one olive, one beige, both with black bands, sat on top of the wardrobe. And Aunt V, standing, or walking a few paces round the centre of the room under the one light-shade, dressed in her brown outside coat, or with that folded across the end of the bed, would squint if she saw him, a cigarette between her fingers, then turn impatiently away.

The only time he ever went into that room was for his birthday. An inadequate florin was searched for in her purse: 'You are eight, fancy,' 'You are nine, well, well,' the words as cold and precise as the coin angled into his palm.

One Saturday afternoon in the long summer holiday, when his mother and Aunt V both were out, he went upstairs.

He didn't go on to his own room. As he stood in her doorway he became afraid that Aunt V would have the magic to still be here though he had seen her go talking and walking up the street with his mother. He pushed the door with his fingertips and it swung slowly inwards. He entered.

The afternoon sun fell through the dusty window onto the wall above the made-up double bed. He looked round. The room was very tall and narrow and empty. On the mantelshelf above the closed-in fireplace was a green glass statuette of a naked woman.

He reached it down. It was heavy and cold. One of the woman's arms was raised, clutched round a fluted pillar. At the top was a candle socket. There was dust inside and under the dust a yellowy-grey resinous caking of dirt and used wax. The glass

woman's hair was parted in the middle, curling in glass waves to
her shoulders. His finger glided over the soft, square face, the
surprisingly sharp pointed nose and lips, to the chest, between the
breasts, over the belly, the channel of thighs and legs, to the heavy
square glass rock- and weed-entangled base.

He carried it to the dressing-table. He sat on the stool and
turned the statuette, watching the face travel slowly round in the
tall mirror. He examined the rest of the table-top.

A snake of blood-red and sea-blue beads veined to look like
stones hung out from an over-full jewellery box. Its lid was inlaid
with mother-of-pearl and sliced wood chess squares. His fingers
fumbled in the box. Under the beads was a silver butterfly, thorax
banded in green and black enamel, wings studded with points of
blue with one missing – a concave lead-gold star. More beads,
black, bright; a string of pearls; a chain of thick, dulled silver
links.

He put the stone beads round his neck. His face looked back
from the mirror. He opened and sniffed warily at a small bottle
with a rubbed label, 'Eau de Toilette'. The yellow-tinged liquid
had a thin, exotic smell. Behind him, in the mirror, the wardrobe
door was closed on a corner of black cloth that stuck out like a
tiny wing.

There were footsteps coming up the stairs. He was almost too
late. As he came through the doorway and ran up the corridor to
his own room he heard her round the stair-head and suck in her
breath.

Through the wall, he heard her moving about, then she came
out of the room and went downstairs again and he heard her voice
raised. He came out on the landing and listened.

'. . . my room . . . my room,' Aunt V was saying. 'Little
enough privacy . . . do what I can . . . If I can't call that my own

. . . boy? Baby, more like . . . oh, yes, baby . . . at nearly eleven.' Her voice rose and fell like a siren.

His mother's answers were muffled and evasive.

'. . . a key . . . a bolt . . .'

'There's no lock – and how can I have a bolt when I am out of the room?'

The atmosphere had stilled and soured when he came down. Aunt V sat behind a magazine. Her lips were pressed so tight together that they had disappeared. When at last she got up and went out of the room, his mother leaned over and whispered.

'Don't go into Aunty's room again, will you, Colin? Not without her permission. She was very upset when she found her things moved around. I don't know . . .'

Aunt V didn't speak to him directly for weeks.

Then Arthur came.

Money had become a problem, it seemed. Whatever Aunt V had had was almost gone. The widow's pension wouldn't keep them. She didn't see how it could keep them. His mother had never worked. 'Your dad didn't want me to,' she explained to Colin. 'He said my job was to look after you. To be here when you came home. He hated an empty house.'

Aunt V said, 'Well, I hope you don't expect me to go to work. Not with my heart.'

Mr Cassell was teaching them French. '*L'horloge sonne trois heures*,' he said. The exam for the grammar was that summer.

His mother had placed an advertisement for a lodger in the local shop. Aunt V only hoped it would be someone suitable. Arthur called on the afternoon she was at the library. He was large and smiling. He was to move in the next day. That afternoon his mother moved her things to Aunt V's room and made up the back bedroom.

'He works in a factory?' Aunt V wailed.

At the first evening meal, she maintained a tight reserve, not looking at the newcomer as he ate slowly and appreciatively. She got up halfway through and said, 'Excuse me, I am going to my room.' Arthur wished her a cheery good-night.

Colin joined her in resisting the newcomer. Arthur tried to be friendly. He was a tall man with a hard body when Colin punched it once, in response at last to the friendly dabs and feints of Arthur's big, deeply stained hands.

By some reversal of what he expected from war, Colin learned that Arthur's wife had been killed at the beginning of '45. 'One of the last,' Arthur said, in his odd, cheerful way. 'V-2. What can you do? It was all like some great bloody silly accident.'

Aunt V pulled a face at the word.

The first night that Arthur took his mother to the pictures, Colin and Aunt V sat on either side of the living-room fire. Aunt V pretended to read a book; Colin could tell because she kept beginning at the top of the same page. She sent him to bed early.

Il est neuf heures moins quart, said Mr Cassell.

She woke him up.

'I never go out. I never go anywhere.' Her voice came through as if she had bored a hole in the wall.

'Well, you never want to,' said his mother.

'Perhaps I was never asked,' said Aunt V.

Arthur bought Aunt V a large box of chocolates with a red bow. She left it untouched on the sideboard. After a week, Arthur broke it open. 'Shame to let them go to waste,' he said.

On Colin's eleventh birthday, Arthur gave him a set of slender, mottled wooden fishing-rods in a long green canvas bag. There was a wicker basket too, with reels, a folded keep net, and hooks and lines neatly packed in tobacco tins.

'They were mine, Col,' said Arthur. 'When I was a lad. I don't get the time now.'

Colin didn't know what to do with the gift. He picked up the rods and they slithered under his fingers in the bag. 'Thank you,' he said.

His mother smiled across at him and said, 'Aunt V wanted us to save them until after the exam. As a reward. But we thought you'd like them now.'

The basket bumped against his legs as he carried the tackle upstairs.

A couple of weeks later the letter arrived. He had not won a scholarship to the grammar school. He had only been offered a fee-paying place.

The uniform had been bought already. The blazer hung in his wardrobe, scarlet, with a unicorned and gryphoned breast-pocket badge shining gold, white and silver. Aunt V caught him in the hallway that afternoon. His mother and Arthur were out.

L'horloge sonne.

'You are a stupid boy. After all we have done for you,' she panted. Her right hand twisted his shoulder, her left plucked at his shirt. 'You have wasted it all. Thrown it away. Now we have to make more money. Make sacrifices. Work because you were idle. Your mother will marry a common little factory worker. He will sleep in your father's bed. And I will be put out.' Her face was huge and he could smell her cold soup breath.

He broke free and ran along the hall and out the front door. Only when he was halfway down the road did he slow to a walk, his tears drying like lead cooling.

That night he stood on the landing again, listening to the row downstairs.

'Canada?' said Aunt V.

'Canada,' said Arthur.

'And what about the boy?' she demanded. 'What is to become of the boy?'

'He'll come with us, of course,' said his mother.

'And what about me?'

There was a silence.

'If we do – then you come too,' said Arthur.

The conversation bubbled on. His mother came into the hall. Colin retreated to his bed.

He lay awake for what seemed a long time, then fell asleep.

What woke him he did not know.

There was no sound in the house. The street-lamp cast a lime-green strip across the ceiling. He got out of bed.

He went out of his bedroom and along the corridor. The hall light had been left on and reflected dimly off the wall onto Aunt V's door and, farther on, the lodger's. He stood in front of Aunt V's for an age.

He twisted the knob slowly, in excruciating silence. He slipped in, pushing the door almost to behind him, but not letting the catch engage.

At first he could see nothing, then a tall rectangle of the wardrobe emerged, the pale oval of the dressing-table mirror, the dark tunnel of the fireplace.

He walked there and reached down the glass statuette from the mantelshelf. It was heavy. To get a better grip he used both hands. He crossed to the bed. There was a dark, indistinct shape on the pillow. He raised the figure, his arms outstretched until it was level with his forehead. He leaned back to increase the momentum of his swing. Then he brought the figure down with all his might.

There was no sound but a dull thud. He hit again. And again.

The door behind him swung open and the light showed the bed. There was something beginning to come from the hair to spread itself on the pillow. And as he looked, another head was raised from the side of that, and Aunt V, dark patterns on her white nightdress, was looking down at the work on the pillow and then back up at him.

'Yes, yes,' she was saying. 'You see what you have done. You have killed your mother. You see what you have done. You have disgraced us. They will hang you. The clock will strike. It is disgrace . . .'

In 1990, in Canada, sweat curled in the hairs on his chest.

'What is it? What's the matter?' Joanne was asking from her sleep.

His eyes focused on the ceiling that was barred with light through the blind's slats.

'Dreaming,' he said. 'I was dreaming I killed Aunt V.'

'Um?'

'Only I didn't.'

'Who?'

'Aunt V. She died years ago.'

'Killed her?'

'It's only a dream. I've had it for years.'

Still half asleep, she looked at his big, sad, pale face.

'Come here,' she said, and reached out. Hooking one arm heavily round his chest she pulled herself to him. 'You're hot as hell,' she said. She went to sleep again.

He lay awake for a while yet, staring at the light on the ceiling, then he too fell asleep.

The Equilibrist

1

Battersea. The boating lake. A numbered boat floats on the grey water, its oars splayed up like twin closed tulips. God, the bus was going the wrong way. Howard hurried down the stairs. Trembling, he walked back a way and caught another bus that would take him safely to the Common.

When he got off again, in Clapham High Street, he noticed that the plate-glass window of the Cypriot's fish and chip shop had once again been shattered. The morose, yellow-faced owner with his black and grey shaving-brush moustache was sweeping the last slivers of glass into a little heap. The man's son – who had served Howard with plaice last week – was incomprehensibly beautiful.

Howard was annoyed with himself that he could not understand more than a few words of the Greek this family spoke among themselves. He stopped. He would address Constantine –

the name above the shop – in the man's forgotten tongue. The tongue of Homer.

'. . . evil lies upon evil,' he stammered. The Cypriot looked up, puzzled. Then shrugged his shoulders and turned away. His beautiful son looked idiotically through the troubled window, invisible hands conjuring fish in batter.

He hurried home to Bel.

Howard lived halfway down one of those roads of stout Edwardian villas that curve away from the south side of Clapham Common. Nothing of interest had happened in the road since one of the Great Train Robbers had lived there in the early sixties. The house had been dismembered by the police. Howard could still see the broken glass, and bricks with plaster and wallpaper still adhering to them, and a lavatory bowl lying broken in the front garden. The windows were long mended; a pot with one green, phallic bulb stood on a delicate table between orange curtains.

He fitted his key into his door. Through the panel of red glass he saw white oblongs of post on the mat.

Inside, he looked through them. Dr Gach. Dr Jan Gach. Mr J. Gach. Mr T. Howard. Not a bill. A cheap white envelope. He put it in his pocket – he would save the opening for upstairs. Something to look forward to.

Howard listened at Gach's door. He could hear nothing. He tried it. Locked. Gach still lectured. Still out.

And just then the sound of a second key ferreting in the front door. Dr Gach let himself in.

A small broad-shouldered man, with a round face, round spectacles behind which were large dark-brown eyes and the lower spikes of thick, grey, tangled eyebrows – the very type of the elderly refugee, protagonist of a thousand and one short stories, Howard had thought the day Gach first came to enquire about renting the bottom floor.

'Mr Howard. How are you?' Gach opened the door of his flat, showing Howard a view of the coloured botanical engravings framed in two neat rows above the fireplace. Books butchered for them, Howard would bet. Despicable habit. He did not like Gach to find him idle at home. Gach the busy bee returning from a full day at college, Surely the man should be retired. Admittedly younger – but he must be sixty-four, five. He looked bloody old.

Howard mounted the stairs as quickly as he could. 'I've been to see my sister,' he announced over his shoulder. 'In Finchley.'

Saving his letter, he put the kettle on. Half a teaspoon of Darjeeling in a mug. Boiling water. When it was ready – tonguing a tiny, soggy twig, spitting it out – he opened the envelope.

It was nonsense.

Who was it from?

A woman in the road. I live in the road, she said. In a comic reflex he almost got up and went to look through the front bedroom window. Eh? Dr Gach had recommended Mr Howard. Atrocious handwriting. Understood he was ex-teacher. Daughter needs a bit of extra tuition for her English exam. Money no matter – but we don't want anything too expensive, naturally.

Naturally. The cheap course – quick trip through the student's notes to *Henry VII*; say what you find to admire in Browning's *Scholar-Gypsy*; in what circumstances does Heathcliff first meet Elinor Dashwood? Stupidity, stupidity. He read on. Perhaps an hour a week. Know your time is your own. As an ex-English teacher . . . An ex-English teacher? An ex-head of department, madam. A deputy head. A man who might . . . given . . . He put the letter down.

Glancing out of the rear window over the garden he saw that

the long grass had been bent down and parted by the morning's hard shower. A wet summer. He switched on the light. T. Howard – no one here had ever known his Christian name. Toby Howard – under his one printed poem. In *The Listener*, June 1937. Never in Grigson's *New Verse*, though he had kept trying. And Toby as a student in Manchester. But Mr Howard, schoolmastering ever since.

And the succession of weeks, months, years, had merged into this unmemorable twist of striped time; day, night, day, night. One evening came back to him – it often came back to him, with increasing vividness. He resented the impertinence of memory. It had been in the week when that publication had given him a legitimate pretension to the title of Poet; he had felt entitled to go to a poet's pub. A pilgrimage that took him into the invisible kingdom of Fitzrovia – that tiny world of pubs and restaurants in the streets around Fitzroy Square. True poets glimpsed boiling and bawling, or broiling and brawling, through the swivelling curate-lights of a bar. The pub was crowded. There was a girl standing behind him. He made way. Her hair, thick and yellow, on which she wore a brown beret. Her eyes were brown, her lips a little thickened and imprecise where her lipstick had smudged. She was extremely beautiful.

'I wonder,' she said, 'if you'd be a love and pass me that.'

'That' was a large pink gin.

He passed over also a light ale for the sullen young man who had huddled in behind her, and a pint of bitter for another who had just arrived.

'I'm awfully sorry, using you as a waiter.' She laughed. 'You don't mind, do you? No. Come and have a drink with us.' The men with her made for a table just vacated. The girl took his arm and led him over. She patted the wall-seat beside her and he sat down. The young man seemed drunk already and said nothing.

The other – who Howard was immediately sure was the girl's lover – had the sandy-pored face of an actor. His handsome profile carried on a conversation with people at the next table. Howard admired the confidence with which the man left his girl with a stranger.

She took a long sip at her drink and set it down. 'What's your name?' she asked.

'Toby. Toby Howard.'

'Oh, that's a lovely name. I'm Bel. B.E.L. What do you do?'

She seemed only faintly less interested when he told her he was a schoolmaster.

'I . . . I do write as well.'

'Ah. You're a poet. Roger's a poet. Aren't you, Roger?'

Roger, the drunken young man, swore as someone, squeezing past the table, trod on his foot. 'Why don't you find somewhere else to bloody go,' he snarled.

'No, not you.' Bel patted Howard's arm. 'Roger's upset because I've left him. He won't leave me. We're at a bit of an impasse.'

Howard smiled weakly, not knowing what to say.

The pub was packed now, and there suddenly came one of those astonishing silences when, coincidentally, everyone stops talking at the same time – and, as suddenly, the hubbub resumed with a burst of laughter. Standing in front of their table was a tiny man in a tweed overcoat that reached almost to the floor.

'Bel!'

'Louis!'

A nod from the lover. A grunt from Roger.

The dwarfish man smiled and bowed his head to kiss Bel's offered hand. He made as if to shake hands with Howard. Howard hesitated. The man withdrew his hand – as Howard advanced his.

'You must have a drink.' Bel began to search in her purse.

'Let me,' Howard protested.

'Would you? Really? You are a darling.'

A Scotch for Louis. A pink gin for Bel – large one, please. A light ale for Roger. A pint for the actor.

It was a struggle to get to the bar. When at last he had been served and battled back with a loaded tray, the drinks lapping and spilling, he saw that Louis had taken his place at Bel's side. They took their glasses and he hung about awkwardly at the table edge for as long as he could. Once or twice Bel looked up and smiled enchantingly at him. But the crush of people eventually forced him away. Then he stood at the bar and waited for one of them, for her, to come to him. In the continuously eddying crowd he was pushed and turned about like a cork float. Roger came to the bar and bought a solitary drink. A large pink gin. He did not look at Howard. And Howard, unaccustomed to the amount of beer he had drunk, went to the Gents. He came back, ordered another drink with great difficulty, turned – and they had gone . . .

He looked round from the window. The flat was silent. The gas fire was beginning to whiten its flames.

Feeling foolish, but none the less determined, he had returned to that pub on the next, Sunday, night. On the following Friday, Saturday and Sunday nights. None of them.

Then, months later, he saw Bel again. Or rather, Bel's picture in *Picture Post*. Her face, cheek-bones moulded by Klieg light, skin stretched like fine suede, was twisted slightly so that she looked down at a bared shoulder. She looked like a goddess. There was no name – the photograph was an advertisement for soap. Sentimentally, he cut it out, mounted it on a piece of card and put it in a silver frame. He wrote her name on the back. Bel.

That was only a year off the war. Mr Howard did not go to the war. Mr Howard was not a hero. The war was a plume of grey smoke that hung into the sky, safely away in the south. From the

school tower one could see the whole conspectus of London –
when he lay down with a book in the warm autumn sun only the
purest blue sky was visible in the mouth of the grey Victorian
mock battlements . . .

There was knocking on his door. It continued.

It was Gach. 'Where haf you been?' Chiding, his ridiculous
accent, his thick, almost pubic eyebrows raised in enquiry – his
whole air of vitality, abruptness, intelligence once more on
display. He had once played chess with Gach and by a lucky,
English game of intuition and unorthodoxy he had defeated him
incredibly quickly – a beautiful, totally unexpected mate. He had
then been made to play five more games, the first lasting over an
hour, the remainder each of decreasing duration, while Gach
exacted his revenge, slowly and intently, bubbling happily into his
extinguished pipe at the end of each victorious game.

'There is someone downstairs.'

'Um,' said Howard. A foot above Gach's left shoulder was the
patch worn by Howard's shoulder where he turned daily on the
stair.

'A Mrs Warrington. She is downstairs,' Gach repeated loudly.
A head appeared at the bottom of the stairwell, the face twisted
upwards.

'Is everything all right?' the woman enquired. Howard's mind
maliciously accentuated the cockney in the woman's voice – is
evryfin' orlrigh'?

'Yes, do come up,' said gentlemanly Dr Gach. Howard
shrugged and went back into his rooms.

'It's-about-my-daughter.' Seating herself, the woman spoke
the words as if demonstrating a classical metre. Dactyl, spondee –
some damn thing. He couldn't remember the difference.

When the girl came to him a few days later, Howard thought her quite pretty but appallingly awkward and ungraceful in her movements. She wore a brown school uniform. He shut the door behind her.

'Do sit down. At the table if you would.'

Her eyes took in the room with half-alarmed contempt: the dust, the books, the few pieces of blue and gold Doulton needing washing, the sepia portraits of his father and mother, incongruous Bel . . .

'All history,' he said. She did not answer.

Her eyes — due, he presumed, to the overbearing sexual self-consciousness of an adolescent — would never quite meet his. She placed a foolscap pad and three books on the table.

'May I?' He reached forward eagerly for the books. They were all modern, or nearly so. *The Lord of the Flies*, *Their Very Own and Golden City*, and a book of poems — who was this? — Seamus Heaney.

'So these are what they have given you to read?'

'Sorry about that.' She giggled.

He looked up sharply, down again, leafing slowly through the poems. They seemed rather old-fashioned, their subject matter mainly agricultural.

'And what do you want to do when you leave school?' He laid the books to one side.

'Not a lot of choice, is there?'

Her air of scornful defeat was irritating. He asked her some elementary questions to test her comprehension of the Golding — the only one he had read. It was not that she was unintelligent — simply that she had no interest in, or rather, no knowledge of any history or tradition that might lie behind these books. Facts were of now and were single, indivisible things to be swallowed — and regurgitated as soon as possible in case they poisoned innocence.

Writers, he suspected, were to her just more teachers in a thin disguise. They broke while he made tea.

As they sat drinking she surprised him with a question. 'What did you want to be? Always a teacher?'

'I haven't been a teacher for years.'

'I suppose not.'

He went on. 'I never regarded myself purely as a teacher. Even when I headed a fairly large department. I – however idle I may be now – regarded myself as a writer. A poet.'

'Why didn't you then? Be a poet?' Her eyes at last looked at him directly.

'It's not quite like that.' Again she had surprised him; by the lack of contempt for the idea in her voice. 'I did publish some poems. One or two. Let me show you something.' He stood up, went across to his desk and pushed up the roller top, still talking.

'When I was in Rome some years ago, oh, quite some years ago – '59, '60 – before you were born – yes, I suppose so – on holiday I saw the great poet Ezra Pound stride with three women and another man across a square. They went into a restaurant. They sat in the window. I almost followed them. It was the nearest I have been to a genius. A sheet of glass. I can still see his magnificent head. No one in those days though, in England certainly, cared or even knew very much about his work.' He had found what he wanted and returned to his chair clutching the postcard with the head of Minerva stamp and Rapallo postmark. 'I wrote to him when I returned to England. How foolish. Sent him some of my own stuff. He was, after all, the only poet I had seen for years. The sight seemed to wake me up. And he was kind enough to write back. You see . . .'

Howard knew the card by heart, but he read it again when she handed it back.

Thangz for POMES
Gut but *dizzy*
Read Bill Williams, Kummingz, Zuk.

'He can't spell either,' she said triumphantly.

'No,' Howard said. 'I suppose he couldn't. But Pound had a vision of Paradise. That is very rare and courageous.'

'Life is bloody hell though, isn't it?'

He was shocked by what she said. He fondled the card for a moment longer. It was obvious it meant nothing to her. She had probably never heard of Pound. He took it back to the desk.

'Life is just a piece of shit, isn't it?' she insisted.

He wheeled round.

'Don't ever say that.'

'Even if it's true?'

'If it is, it is our duty to pretend otherwise.'

'Pretend?'

'To live otherwise.'

She looked hostilely at him. Something must be done.

'It's time, I think, for us to get on with the work your mother is paying for, don't you?'

When she had gone he realized how feeble his answers had been. He should have been more positive. Whatever she – or he, for that matter – felt should have been further explored. To persuade her – to what? Perhaps life was like that.

'I did not mean to say that. It would be wicked,' he said aloud. Bel stared down at her shoulder. It was, he thought, like Dylan Thomas calling himself a dog. Wishing to be a dog, even in fun. It was blasphemous to wish away our humanity. To be an animal. 'We shall all be that soon enough.' The room did not answer, except that the curtains, as if full of some life, billowed and resettled in the draught from the open window.

2

A child, you gazed into the long cheval glass and the reflected window showed the garden beyond. You moved closer and each leaf, blade of grass, spike of hawthorn retreated, edged by its own glassy ghost, into the depths of the mirror.

In Cocteau's film the young man, hair combed neatly back, dressed in a double-breasted suit, walks through the mirror, which melts and reforms like water around him . . .

On the other side of the mirror, nose pinched, eyes flat and pale, Howard. The evening bled, reddening his thin grey hair.

Yet the shock diminished. His seventy-year-old face made excuses for itself the longer he regarded it.

There was someone knocking on the door.

He did not recognize her at first. The gawky, angular girl in the school uniform had become a rounded female torso borne on long, white-stockinged legs and surmounted by a Coppelian doll's head with a large orange spot on each white powdered cheek.

'Hello, Mr Howard.'

'I didn't know it was you for a moment.'

'It's Saturday.'

That presumably was explanation enough.

'Ah. Sit down. I was just about to make a drink.'

'I can't stay long, Mr Howard,' she said, but in the kitchen he did not hear her. When he came back in he remembered something else.

'You . . . in the week . . . I wanted you to see another thing . . .' He went to the desk again. 'It's years since I last looked at it myself.' He held up a worn loose-leaf binder. A white label had been pasted on and a title written in his neat italic hand. She squinted, trying to read what it said.

'What is it?'

'A book. A short book.' He began already to feel a little foolish, to wish the girl gone; for him to be alone with the book, with . . . 'It is something I wrote many years ago.' He looked down at the folder. Oh Bel, this was for you. Not this other.

'What's it about?'

'About? It is not *about* anything. It is about the impossibility of love. The implausibility, if you like.'

She stared at him. He almost laughed – it was impossible for her to envisage himself as a lover.

Quite right, too.

'Why is it called that?' She pointed to the label. 'What does it mean?'

'Ah. From a poem by John Crowe Ransom. I use the last verse as an epigraph.'

He opened the folder and in his high, precise voice he read:

> Equilibrists lie here; stranger, tread light;
> Close, but untouching in each other's sight;
> Mouldered the lips and ashy the tall skull,
> Let them lie perilous and beautiful.

As he read he rocked slowly back and forth on his heels.

'An equilibrist,' he explained, 'is a tightrope walker – or perhaps one who prefers always a safe equilibrium, a state of emotional balance – it is a deadly pun.'

It was difficult for her, he saw, to be enthusiastic about his history, his dream . . . Perhaps – how awful – she thought he had been boasting.

'Hard to write about love. Your youth does not permit . . . I suppose though that in the end I hadn't the talent.' He found himself staring down at her thighs. She tugged the short skirt forward. 'The finer things . . .'

'Look, I only really came for the book I left. I've really got to be going.'

Two days later, expecting the girl that evening, he received instead a letter. Delivered by hand evidently, as there was no stamp. Pushed through the letterbox downstairs. Brought up by Dr Gach.

And when Gach stood in the doorway holding out the envelope it was, Howard supposed, necessary to invite him in. The dishes of last night's meal still littered the table.

'Excuse me, I have no cat,' said Howard.

Gach looked puzzled.

'To dispose of the remains of the fish.' Howard chuckled as if he had caught out the clever Dr Gach – the Herr Doktor. And Gach – not a doctor of medicine, but with a doctorate in the sciences – thought that Howard was perhaps a little odder than usual today.

'Men like us should have wives,' he joked.

Howard did not apparently hear. He thrust the letter back towards Gach. 'I don't understand it. What does she say?'

Gach read. The woman, it seemed, was not happy with the tuition her daughter had been receiving and she thought that Mr Howard had wasted their time. Also she did not think it right that a man of his age should talk to a young girl about 'love and things'. Thank you, but she won't come again. Yours faithfully.

'I don't think your pupil is coming back,' said Gach, refolding the letter. 'It is extraordinary, don't you think,' he mused, 'that after more than a hundred years of compulsory education a middle-aged Englishwoman cannot form a single correct sentence?'

'It is not important,' said Howard, 'whether she comes or not.

She was not entirely stupid – but what is to be done with such people?' He began to stack the dishes.

Gach laid the letter on a small table by the door.

'Quite,' he said.

Howard went out to the kitchen.

Gach heard water begin to splash into a bowl. 'I do have an appointment,' he said loudly. But there was no response except for the clattering of washing-up. Gach went out, closing the door slowly, looking back into the room for a moment.

3

One morning Howard woke and it was winter.

Then it seemed he was living in Hell. That it was an actual locality bounded by the walls that arranged themselves – the B of the front bedroom bays mating with the elongated L of the living-room, kitchen and bathroom – to form the first letters of some mad alphabet.

The winter was unremittingly severe. For weeks, not days, snow lay compacted on the pavements and in huge drifts filled the small, low-walled front gardens. A livid gleam clung all day to the ceilings as if light itself had become glassy and hard.

The trees and roofs at the rear looked spectacularly, crystallinely beautiful. He said, 'Bel, come and see this.' She sat in the pale cold light a little way into the room. She did not get up to come and look at what he wanted her to admire. 'Bel . . .'

For the first time he cursed her. He raged. 'All this romantic shit, these airs and bloody graces – earth, flesh, mud, filth.' Bel looked mutely down at her grey shoulder.

The beauty of the snowscape became monotonous; the eternal glare from the snow hurt his eyes, its luminescence haunting his rooms even on moonless nights.

Gach pushed a card through the door but Howard did not pick

it up from the floor. Nothing seemed important enough to bother with – or rather everything seemed momentously unimportant. In a routine he established of rising late, making tea, shaving slowly – interminably – of sitting by the fire all day, of visits, essential but exhausting, to the shops, of retiring early to bed, any deviation became a maddening irritation. He did not want to read. His one intelligent pastime was to sit at the front bedroom window and watch the occasional stranger walking gingerly in the road, the cars that followed like crabs, their rear ends sliding sideways on the ice.

At last the snow on the pavements began to fall away, the channels that shoes had worn revealing tiny stones, dead insects and leaves held in the underlying ice. The garden drifts rounded and showed blue shadows where the snow beneath had begun to collapse. Emerging from its long sleep, the upstairs flat was a disgrace. For the whole of the winter he had not cleaned or tidied. Ashamed, the first day that the sun shone warmly through the window he spent half an hour wrestling until he managed to raise the lower sash. In the cold air he cleaned and tidied. Birds sang. The room grew radiantly around him.

His face, reflected in the blue window as the bus swung across the bridge in sunlight, disappeared again as they plunged into the triangular shadow between warehouses. The girls in the street had cockatoo hair of orange and yellow-green, short skirts . . .

His sister, Edith, lived on the wrong side of Kensington Gardens.

'But souf ov ve 'Arrow Road, ducks,' she used to say, affecting an appalling cockney accent, chiding him for his snobbishness.

'I am not a snob.' His face reddened. 'It is impossible for me to have been a snob,' he said loudly. The upper deck of the bus was almost empty.

He looked out for his usual alighting point – a corner restaurant.

The bus was passing through Paddington when he realized he had not seen it, should have, and that this was much too far on. He got off at the next stop and walked back. It took a long time and when he arrived the roads curved in unfamiliar ways around the accustomed corner. The café was no longer there. A garage. A low block of flats in the approved children's drawing style – with scissored oblong windows and crayoned walls. The aerosoled graffiti were large, red and black, runic in their unintelligibility. A crone hurried children across the road, threatening them with an orange, bulbous wand. This manic clowness waved him back as he attempted to cross.

In the topography of a dream all is familiar, and irresistibly altered. He walked down this street, up that; scenting with keen terror that what he sought was hidden, always about to be grasped, but slipping insistently away, unseen, round each corner he approached.

At last, a street of small shops and terraced houses that he recognized. The church of their childhood rose up. What had happened? The gates were hung with chains. Planks of wood were nailed across the double doors, and in the long windows on either side of the porch many small lozenges of glass had been broken, to leave hollow lead diamonds full of dust and extinguished light.

He hurried into the side-street where Edith lived. Halfway down, a forty-foot-high concrete curtain fell. On it the tops of cars could be seen gliding; into it disappeared the frieze of Greek-key-patterned tiles that ran along the faces of the houses. This monstrous wall hid – had absorbed – his sister's house. The remaining houses were boarded up; the long, rather charmingly genteel street had become this horrific cul-de-sac.

Disturbed, he made his way back to the main road.

'Excuse me . . .' The man he addressed walked by without answering. The next to be approached, a woman, backed away, plainly scared when he attempted to detain her by grabbing her sleeve. She seemed even more frightened when he repeated his question.

'Excuse me, could you please tell me . . .'

The household rubbish was not taken down by Howard that week. Nor the next. He left the black bags outside his door, open, not with the neat rabbit-ears' knots he normally tied to seal them. The absence of Howard, and the sweet, sick odour of decaying food led Gach upstairs. He had to twist, lips pursing in distaste, round the bags on the small landing.

When Howard at last answered his insistent knock, he did not appear to recognize Gach.

'Mr Howard?'

'Yes?'

'Dr Gach. Are you all right?'

'Oh yes, Dr Gach.' Howard blinked; he had a week's growth of sandy-grey beard. 'Come in. Come in.'

The table was covered with soiled plates and cups, a sauce bottle fallen on its side. The carpet was speckled with crumbs, a milk-bottle top had been flattened into the thin pile like an ancient silver coin.

'You're not well, Mr Howard?'

'Perhaps you would like some tea?' said Howard with a thin-voiced, studied politeness. But he made no move to get tea or do anything else, but simply stared down at the floor.

Gach said, 'Sit down. Please. I will get the tea for us.'

Howard looked round the room as if it was he who had been invited in, then sat abruptly down on the chair at the end of the table. 'Yes, perhaps. If you would. That would be most kind.'

The kitchen was squalid. There were piles of unwashed dishes in the sink, opened tins on the table, some of the contents only half consumed, with the remainders moulded over. Gach washed two cups vigorously, found some tea-bags and set the kettle to boil. There was silence from the other room.

He came back in with the cups, forcing himself to smile cheerfully. He set one in front of Howard.

Howard stared fixedly down, not touching the tea. Then he looked; his hands in his lap twisted together in a hard ball on the table.

'Trouble is, Gach, we're at the business end of life. Eh?'

Gach laughed uncertainly. 'I suppose so. Now, please, drink your tea. It will make you feel better.'

'Gach, what is happening to me?' said Howard; his hands came apart, trembling, then reknotted more fiercely than before. His jaw worked as if he was chewing air. 'I feel like a child. As if my life should be beginning. Instead of this!'

He shot up from the chair, then sat slowly again as Gach, laying his own cup carefully on the table, leaned over the corner of the table, holding Howard's arms gently and lowering him down. Gach waited for a moment and then said, 'You are not well, Mr Howard. Is there someone I can get for you? Your sister perhaps? You go to see her, don't you?'

'She wasn't there. I didn't understand . . .'

'You have her address. Her telephone number? You have an address book?'

'In the bureau. There's a book.'

'I'll get it,' said Gach gently. 'Now – you sit there. Drink.'

He went to the bureau. There was a small red leather-covered address book just inside. He carried it back to the table.

'May I bring her for you?'

'I want to see no one,' said Howard in a high, testy voice. 'I want only to be left alone.'

'Yes, yes. I shall be just downstairs if you should want me. I shall take this. Yes?' Gach left Howard, bent forward in the chair, seeming to stare into some inconceivably deep well.

The book was no help. There was no other Howard in the sprinkling of names. Presumably the sister had married; Gach had no idea which of the numbers to ring. He put the book down. He listened. There was no sound from upstairs. Something must be done. Feeling guilty, as if he were somehow betraying Howard, he picked up the phone and asked for directory inquiries.

A little after noon the next day a small red Japanese car drew up outside. Gach opened the door on a young woman wearing enormous spectacles that almost covered her small face.

'Mr Gach?'

'Doctor,' he corrected her.

'No, I am not a doctor,' she said patiently. 'Social Services. You rang us.'

He began to explain about Howard, finding himself excusing the man's state, wishing this woman elsewhere. She asked if Howard had any relatives. Anyone they could contact? He handed her the address book. She flicked through and put it into the thick buff manilla folder she carried.

'Mr Howard is upstairs?' she asked brightly.

He offered to lead the way, but she had already started up the stairs, saying she would find her own way, thanks, acknowledging his help with a wave of the folder.

Only a couple of minutes later Gach heard Howard's door open and the sound of his voice shouting. Then the door slammed to again. The young woman came down the stairs, briskly, but

calmly enough. As he opened the door she said, 'There shouldn't
be any difficulty. I'll try and be back tomorrow. You will be in?'

At five the day after, the car returned. Gach watched through
his net curtain. There was a passenger this time; an older woman.
Almost as the younger woman rapped on the door, Gach opened
it.

'This is Mr Howard's sister.'

The women sat among Gach's plants and books.

'I cannot understand what he was doing there,' said Howard's
sister; she had the same face, if anything a stronger, more
determined face, the only feminine aspect her bush of thick grey
hair. 'We haven't lived there since long before the war.'

'A momentary lapse perhaps . . .' said Gach consolingly.

A dull scraping came from the room above, as if a table was
being dragged across the floor.

'Who is Bel?' asked the sister the next day.

The young woman in glasses was inserting Howard into the
rear of the car.

'Pardon?' said Gach, turning away from the window.

She held out the photograph she had found among Howard's
papers.

'I'm afraid I don't know. Someone he knew?'

'I would hardly think so.'

'No.'

'My brother was not particularly interested in women.' She
looked at the picture again. 'It does not seem right to throw it
away, though. The frame is a good one. Perhaps you could find a
use for it.'

'Your brother, surely?'

'No.'

Reluctantly he took it from her.

The horn sounded from outside.

'I will call back if there is anything else. Thank you.'

How long have you lived here, Dr Gach? But she did not ask that. They shook hands and she went out to the car.

At last the house was still. She would probably sell it now that she and Howard were to live together.

He laid the photograph face down on the window-sill and made his way back to his kitchen. He looked out to where Howard's sister had this morning held a bonfire of old clothes and papers that Howard, she said, would no longer be needing. The fire smouldered still under the ashes and a little fugitive smoke hung across the dark bushes at the end of the garden.

Performer, Performance

Snow fell into the club entrance. The warm air from inside died before it reached the edge of the scarlet carpet. McKendrew leaned out to look up the street.

At last a car turned from the orange glow of the main road and moved down. The wheels hobbled on crusts of ice. It stopped at the entrance.

The driver got out. He read the neon sign high on the wall, smacked the top of the car, and called across to McKendrew, 'Hide yourself away a bit up here, don't you?' He came around to open the rear door and bent to look inside. 'We're there,' he said.

The passenger got slowly out, drawing a long brown leather case after him.

In the club's foyer a large photograph on an easel showed a broad-shouldered, middle-aged black man, his arms cradling a saxophone, a faintly malicious smile on his huge, handsome face.

But the man on the pavement seemed to barely fill his clothes.

He was bald, with a few wisps of white hair straggling to his collar; the heavy-lidded eyes were thinned to slits, his skin yellow. He shivered and folded a long, opulent, ancient fur coat about him.

'I'll have to have a signature.' The driver had brought out a tattered duplicate book.

The passenger had gone into the entrance and stood, looking round slowly; at the carpet, the walls, the ceiling.

'To prove you've had him,' said the driver. 'They get lost sometimes on these out-of-town jobs. Or just don't turn up. This one hasn't said a word all the way up.'

McKendrew signed and tore off his copy. He ground it in his fist and let it fall to the snow.

The driver was getting back into the car. 'I'll pick him up at about one,' he said. 'Wants to go back to the city. Can't say I blame him.'

In the foyer, the old man stood in front of the easel, the case clutched in one hand, the long fingers of the other stroking his cheek as he looked at the photograph.

McKendrew strode past him and opened one of the double doors into the club. 'Come in,' he said. With an odd, shuffling walk, the man followed him.

Heavy drapes hung down the windowless walls of the converted warehouse. Between the drapes were pasted huge black and white photographs of famous jazz musicians; after five years they had turned a dingy, nicotine-stained grey-yellow. A false ceiling extended as far as the band-stand. To the side, steps led to the mezzanine dining area, 'The Bistro'.

'Mr Alex asked me to look after you till he got here,' said McKendrew. 'He'll be late. I'll show you to the office.'

An hour later the phone rang.

'Mr Alex. Half-past six when he came,' said McKendrew.

'OK. No, nothing to eat. Just sat down in the office and put the fire on and asked for a bottle of brandy. Rémy Martin. That's all he said. So I got him that. I made a bill out but he just put it in his pocket. Eh? All right. If that's all right with you? Yeah, yeah — we'll look after him.'

The phone must have rung and rung up in the office; McKendrew had been called at last to the extension in 'The Bistro'. The little restaurant, with Chianti bottles hanging from the blue-lit fishing nets on the walls, was empty.

But the club floor was filling up rapidly. Wednesday night was usually dead, but not this one.

And the crowd coming in were older than usual. They were dressed in sports coats and cords, or smart suits a few years out of fashion. There were not so many women, and they weren't young either. McKendrew made his way through them all, proud of the way the swagger of his broad, powerful body made them part, amused as one of them bumped into him and spilled a spot of beer-froth on his shoe and then began apologizing profusely as McKendrew stared hard down at him.

Passing the bar, he nodded to the girls serving. They laughed at him, he knew that. At his belly and balding crew-cut. They didn't know what a man was . . .

He went up the uncarpeted stairs to the office.

The old man sat on a straight chair, hunched over the electric fire. On the wall above him the calendar had only one month left, December 1967. McKendrew looked at his watch. After nine. Mr Alex had said he was on his way over. Time to work. He coughed loudly and took a step forward.

'Is it time?' the slurred, thick voice asked. 'Give me that, will you?' He pointed to the case on the desk. Beside it, the brandy bottle had about an inch left in it.

Opening the case, the man took out the shining trunk and neck of a tenor saxophone. His hands were steady as he assembled the instrument, putting on the mouthpiece, mulling over a box of reeds, wetting one between his lips, then screwing up the ligature with strong fingers. He pushed out his lower lip, his thick tongue wetted the reed once more. He reared his head back and regarded the mouthpiece. He adjusted it slightly, then applied his lips again, twiddled a couple of keys exploratively, and gave out a great, sudden blast of sound.

'Christ,' said McKendrew. 'Makes hell of a noise, don't she?'

Alex had arrived. He was a disappointed man. It had always been his dream to bring great jazz names – the names he had learned off record sleeves in his youth – to play in his club. He'd kept a jazz policy going as long as he could, but lately fees had been too high, attendances sparse, the artists unreliable . . . The rock boom was sweeping everything else out of the clubs.

'What's it like?' he asked McKendrew.

'Full,' said his doorman.

Surprised by the crush, Alex eased his way to the front.

The rhythm section had started to play already. A long, long introduction to a blues. The great tenor saxophone player hugged the crook of the hired grand piano, smiling to himself, eyes hooded, swaying slightly, disinclined to join in.

Alex was shocked by the man's appearance. Of course he'd heard rumours – of drink and illness, that he wasn't playing well on this tour with local scratch trios, and the man was in his sixties – but the rumours didn't prepare you for the fall, for the once-powerful body shrunk in the too-large suit, the shirt collar awry, the loud painted silk tie falling out of the buttoned jacket.

In Alex's head, in the heads of the audience, were all the legends of this man. He had played with Bessie Smith and Billie Holiday, guested imperiously with Ellington and Basie, Charlie

Parker and Coltrane. He had invented the saxophone as a jazz instrument the same way Armstrong had invented the trumpet. All their heads rehearsed his old solos . . .

He cradled the saxophone in his arms. His head nodded in and out of time to the music; the pianist kept looking up at him, waiting for, and not getting, some sign. At last, with infinite weariness, the man lifted the saxophone to his mouth.

The sound faltered and wheezed; for a terrible moment Alex feared that his performer was not going to be able to play at all. Then the notes fattened and grew rich, until it was as if a huge, extraordinarily beautiful rose had unfurled, filling the room. In Alex, the music spread along his veins like another blood. The old man disappeared; there was only the great, soft sound that whispered, boomed, cried out, sang and, above all, spoke of love. Then it stopped, and the old man was looking at the ecstatically applauding audience as if it did not exist.

In the office, Alex counted money into the outstretched hand. He tried again to put his thanks into words. 'Wonderful. Absolutely wonderful. Thanks so much for coming . . .' – words which seemed utterly inadequate as repayment for the two hours of power and beauty which had been given tonight. The player simply grunted, stowing the money carefully in an inner pocket of the fur coat. Alex was ashamed to feel relieved when McKendrew came in to say the car was here. The old man drained the last of his glass slowly.

'The case,' he said.

McKendrew carried it down the stairs, feeling resentment at having to do this thing. What in God's name Mr Alex saw in these old blacks he couldn't guess.

He stowed the case in the back of the car and held the door open. The driver yawned.

'Thank you again for coming,' said Alex. 'It was wonderful. Truly wonderful . . .'

The old man's handshake was brief and slack. He sat in the back of the car and stared straight in front.

The car started forward; the rear wheels raced in the snow, the driver spinning the wheel to turn in the narrow street. It lurched forward again and then went slowly forward up to the main road. At the top it hesitated, turned again, and went away from the town.

Alex dropped the empty brandy bottle into the waste-paper basket. Marvellous night; but he had still lost money on it. Jazz sold too much beer; too much attention was given to the artist. You sold far more with the movement and youth of the disco.

So that one was the last. The jazz was over. He felt suddenly depressed; he could do with a drink himself. A large Scotch. He sat behind the desk. On the cassette player was a tape of the great saxophonist. He switched it on. It had been recorded sometime in the '50s. The tune was fast, the saxophone lunged and flashed arrogantly through a barrage of riffing brass. For some reason the very vigour of the playing was profoundly dispiriting. Alex turned it off abruptly.

In the bar McKendrew heard the music start, charge forward for a minute, then stop. He pulled the bar shutters rattling down. He came out and locked the door, leaving one light shining weakly on the mirrored bottles.

The empty floor was scuffed and dirty. Moving his powerful arms easily into the swing, he began to pile chairs up on tables, whistling tunelessly as he worked his way along to the dark bandstand.